Pantomime
PONIES

GILLIAN BAXTER

Pantomime
PONIES

Illustrated by Elisabeth Grant

MAMMOTH

Also by Gillian Baxter

Ponies in Harness
Ponies by the Sea
Save the Ponies!

First published in Great Britain 1969
by Methuen & Co Ltd
Methuen Paperback edition first published 1977
Published 1994 by Mammoth
an imprint of Reed Consumer Books Ltd
Michelin House, 81 Fulham Road, London SW3 6RB
and Auckland, Melbourne, Singapore and Toronto

Text copyright © 1969 Gillian Baxter
Illustrations copyright © 1969 Elisabeth Grant

ISBN 0 7497 1729 7

A CIP catalogue record for this title
is available from the British Library

Printed and bound in Great Britain
by Cox & Wyman Ltd, Reading, Berkshire

Contents

1 · Uncle Arthur

Ian and Angela Kendall gazed anxiously out of the taxi window as it turned yet another corner. The street was still drab and grey, as all the streets had been since they left the High Street, but here there was a little more life about it. People were walking to and from a short row of shops at the farther end, and the lights in the shop windows glowed warmly in the damp, grey dusk.

"Do you think one of those is Uncle Arthur's shop?" asked Angela.

"I should think so," replied Ian. "Aunt Mavis said that he'd got a paper shop."

Angela was silent again, as the taxi slowed down to swing across the road. She had long fair hair and her eyes were blue, and at the moment her face was pale and nervous. She was eight years old, and Ian, who looked very much like her, was nine. Their mother and father had died so long ago that Angela could not even remember them. Ian said that he could remember their mother, but Angela did not think that he could, although she enjoyed listening to his stories about her.

It was the thought of another new home, although a temporary one this time, that was making Angela nervous. She and Ian seemed to have had so many. Since their parents died they had lived with Grandmother, with Auntie Lorna and Uncle Sam, with Cousin John and Aunt Carrie, and with Aunt Mavis. And now that Aunt Mavis had gone to Ashby to look after her mother, who had fallen and broken an ankle, they were to stay here in south east London with Uncle Arthur until she returned. It seemed an awful lot of homes in less than eight years.

The taxi stopped outside the first shop in the row, the paper shop. A board above the door read "A. Perry. Newsagent, Tobacconist and Confectioner". In the lighted window were boxes and jars of sweets, packets of cigarettes, tins of tobacco, magazines, cake-decorations, and plastic toys. It was the first week of January, and the Christmas decorations were still up. Blobs of cotton wool were stuck to the glass, and strands of tinsel hung behind the goods on display. It was rather a haphazard sort of window, looking as though someone had arranged it in a frightful hurry. On either side of the door, racks held copies of evening and local papers, and there was a board behind the glass in the door for small postcard advertisements.

"Here you are, then," the taxi driver told them. "Shall I take your stuff inside?"

"We'd better ask, first," replied Ian, and he and Angela climbed out.

The shop bell jangled loudly as Ian pushed open the door, and Angela followed him uncertainly inside. The shop was very small, with two counters: one for sweets, cigarettes, and oddments, the other for newspapers and magazines. Paper chains hung across the ceiling, and there was a cluster of balloons suspended over the door. In spite of the noise from the bell, no one appeared.

"I'll try the bell again," said Ian.

He opened and closed the door again, with the same loud jangle, but still nobody came.

"Had we better try knocking on the other door?" asked Angela. There was an inner door, with a piece of green curtain hung over the glass in the top half.

They were about to try this idea when the shop door opened, and a woman came in. She was short and stout, dressed in a black coat, bedroom slippers, and curlers under a head scarf.

"No one about?" she asked them cheerfully.

"No," replied Angela.

"He'll be out the back," the woman told them.

Without hesitation she went behind the counter, opened the inner door, and yelled "Arthur. Shop." Then she came back and leaned against the counter, beaming at them.

"You'll be Cousin Jack's kids, come to stay," she said. "Angela and Ian. You've had him in a right state, I can tell you."

"We have? Why?" asked Angela.

"Arthur looking after kids?" the woman laughed. "Frightened him to death. He's probably hiding out there now."

There was a sound of hurried footsteps beyond the inner door, then it swung open, and Uncle Arthur came hurriedly into the shop. He was a tall, thin, red-faced man with grey hair going rather thin on top, blue eyes, and bushy grey eyebrows.

"Sorry, May," he began. "I was just. . . ." Then he noticed the two children, and stopped short.

"The kids are here, Arthur," the woman told him. "Angela and Ian. Thought you'd run off or something."

She laughed again, and Uncle Arthur's face became redder.

"Oh my goodness," he exclaimed. "I am sorry. I wasn't expecting you just yet. Your

11

luggage. What about your luggage?"

"It's outside," Ian told him. "The taxi's still here. Shall we let the driver bring it in?"

"Yes, yes, of course. Better use the side door. Awkward through here," said Uncle Arthur. "May, would you mind? Just a few minutes. Shan't be long."

"I don't mind," May assured him.

Uncle Arthur followed Angela and Ian outside, showed the taxi driver the side door, and then hurried back into the shop to unlock it. Angela and Ian looked at each other uncertainly. Uncle Arthur seemed awfully disorganised. And was it true that their coming had really scared him? The other relations that they had stayed with had sometimes been unwelcoming, or irritable, but never scared.

The side door opened with a jerk, and the driver carried their cases into the narrow passage, before returning to his taxi. Uncle Arthur led the way down the passage, past some stairs, and into the back room.

"Must just see to the shop. Make yourselves at, er, home," he told them, and vanished through the green-curtained door. Angela and Ian looked around them.

Uncle Arthur's living-room was different from anywhere that they had stayed before. To start with it was very crowded, while Aunt Mavis's home had been spacious and tidy. Chairs, tables, a sagging settee, a huge sideboard, an ornate upright piano, and towering shelves of books fought each other for space. A blue budgerigar in a big cage chattered above them, his cage suspended from a hook in the ceiling. A hot coke fire burned in the grate, and there was a huge ginger cat spread out on the hearth in front of it.

On the mantelpiece, on top of the sideboard, and all round the room were photographs and old playbills of music hall performances and circuses. Many of the photographs were signed, and looked like old-fashioned film stars.

Out in the shop the bell jangled as May

13

went out, and Uncle Arthur came back into the room. He beamed at them rather anxiously, and said, "Well. So you're Angela and Ian?"

"Yes," agreed Ian.

"Isn't he a lovely cat," said Angela. Usually she was very shy, but knowing that their uncle was shy of them made it somehow easier to talk to him.

"Oh yes. Partner. He helps me run the shop. The mice are his department," replied Uncle Arthur.

The ginger cat raised his head at the sound of his name, and stared at the children with large golden eyes.

"Well now," Uncle Arthur started towards the passage door, "we'd better take your luggage upstairs. See your rooms."

The stairs were very steep and narrow, and led on to a tiny landing with a door on either side. Ian and Uncle Arthur struggled with the cases, and Angela followed.

"On the left," instructed Uncle Arthur.

The room had been divided at some time

14

by a hardboard partition which did not quite reach to the ceiling. Half of the window was in each half of the room, and each part contained a bed, a chest of drawers, and a curtained corner for hanging suits and dresses. There was a rag rug beside each bed.

"Not what you're used to, I expect?" said Uncle Arthur. He bounced one of the beds up and down anxiously, and Angela said, "It's lovely. Does it matter which half we choose?"

"No, up to you," replied Uncle Arthur. "Er, well, come down when you're ready. Bathroom's downstairs. Had it built on."

He went off with obvious relief, and Ian and Angela looked at one another.

"I like him," said Angela decidedly. "He isn't like the others."

"No, he isn't," agreed Ian. "It might be fun here."

They unpacked a few of their things, and then went downstairs. There was a strong smell of cooking, and a haze of blueish

15

smoke was drifting in through a door on the far side of the living room. Angela and Ian went to investigate, and found Uncle Arthur cooking sausages in a small, surprisingly bare kitchen.

"Hope you like sausages?" asked Uncle Arthur.

"Oh, we do," Angela assured him.

The sausages were well cooked by the time Uncle Arthur put them on the table. They were so well cooked that half of them were black, and Angela wondered if all Uncle Arthur's cooking was like this. If so, she would ask if she could do some herself, for her mistakes would hardly matter. She might even manage to do better.

There was plenty of bread and butter to eat with the sausages, and a luscious cherry cake to follow. Angela and Ian wondered where it had come from. It seemed too good to be from a shop, and it did not seem likely that Uncle Arthur had cooked it himself.

While they ate Uncle Arthur asked rather stiffly polite questions about Aunt Mavis, and

16

how they got on at school. It was still the holidays at present, but if Aunt Mavis had to stay away for very long they would go to school near Uncle Arthur's. There had been some talk about them being sent to boarding schools, but Aunt Mavis had decided that they were not really old enough yet. Also a boarding school would be expensive, and Angela and Ian knew that their aunt was not very well off, in spite of her beautifully kept and furnished home. Aunt Mavis had said that she might try to get Ian into a State boarding school later on.

The shop bell rang several times during tea, and Uncle Arthur went to serve the customers. Partner sat by his master's chair, waiting regally to be handed bits of sausage and cake.

After the meal the children helped their uncle to wash up, and then he went to close the shop. He came back into the living room beaming and rubbing his hands.

"No more demands tonight," he said. "Open at eight tomorrow. Now, time you met the rest of the family."

Angela and Ian looked up in surprise. There was no one else in the house, and Partner and the bird, Bluey, had already been introduced to them. What more family could Uncle Arthur have? But their uncle was putting on an old jacket which hung behind the kitchen door, and taking a large, red, electric lamp down from the top of the dresser.

"Better slip your coats on," he told them. "Bit chilly down the yard."

Angela and Ian did so, and followed Uncle Arthur down two steps into the dark yard. There was a high fence on either side of them, and the backs of other houses faced them, with lights in many of the windows. Further away, a towering, skyscraper block of offices loomed against the sky, many of its windows still lighted. Behind it the night sky was pink and luminous with the lights of London.

Uncle Arthur's lamp showed them a long shed with a slanting roof built against the wall at the end of the yard. There was also a gate in this wall. It was only a few steps from the house to the shed, and when Uncle Arthur's hand touched the door latch there was a rustling noise inside, and something made a soft, deep, blowing sound.

"Hello then. I've brought you some visitors," said Uncle Arthur, opening the door. "Not fans yet, but they soon will be."

Angela and Ian followed him into the shed, and Angela gave a small shriek of delighted surprise. The shed was divided into two halves by poles and wooden partitions, and in each half was a tiny, cream-coloured pony with a flowing mane and tail and big, dark eyes.

"Magic and Moonshine," said Uncle Arthur. "My pantomime stars."

"Pantomime?" asked Ian. "Do you mean they go on the stage? Like at the Palladium?"

"Just like that," agreed Uncle Arthur. "Mind you, we haven't quite made the Palladium yet, but there's time. At the moment we're appearing at the Corry Empire, in

19

'Cinderella'. Got Donnie Shaw as Buttons."

"Donnie Shaw? The one who makes records?" asked Ian.

"That's right," agreed Uncle Arthur.

Angela was stroking the ponies, who had both thrust their noses over the partitions, and were nuzzling her gently.

"Which is Magic and which is Moonshine?" she asked.

"The one on the left is Magic," replied Uncle Arthur. "He's got a star on his forehead, look, and he's a bit smaller than Moonshine."

There was a white, star-shaped marking on Magic's forehead, and he was more pushful than Moonshine. The shed smelt sweetly of fresh hay and straw, and clean horse, and the light from the lamp showed bales of hay stacked in the space between the two partitions. Partner had followed them from the house, and now he jumped up on to Moonshine's partition. The pony nuzzled him with a gentle nose, and the big cat rubbed his whiskers against the pony.

"They're great friends," said Uncle Arthur. "Partner often sleeps on Moonshine's back if he wants a nap in the day."

"When are they in the pantomime?" asked Ian.

"Every night except Sunday and Monday," replied Uncle Arthur. "It's Monday today, of course. There isn't much of a house on Monday, so they don't open tonight."

Two short poles at one end of each partition took down to make a doorway, and Uncle Arthur lowered Magic's top pole.

"Shake hands with the lady, Magic," he instructed.

Solemnly, Magic lifted one forefoot, and offered it to Angela. She took it in her hand, feeling the cool hardness of the pony's narrow leg. His ankles, or fetlocks, as she later learned to call them, were little thicker than her own wrist. Not wanting to be left out, Moonshine too was lifting his forefoot in the air, and Ian shook hands with him between the poles.

21

"Can they do a lot of tricks?" Angela asked Uncle Arthur.

"Oh, a good few, a good few," replied Uncle Arthur.

"Did you teach them?" Ian wanted to know.

"Oh, er, well, yes, I did," Uncle Arthur looked embarrassed. "Always have liked to have an animal to train, you know. I used to have a dog, big Collie. He was never as good as these, though."

He refilled Moonshine's water-bucket at a tap in the yard outside, and gave both ponies a large armful of hay.

"That's it until tomorrow, then," he told Angela and Ian. "Come along. Now, what about your bedtimes?"

2 · Magic and Moonshine

In spite of being in strange beds, Angela and Ian both slept well that night. They were woken while it was still dark the next morning by the sound of Uncle Arthur moving about downstairs, and by shrill whistles as the paper boys arrived. While they were getting dressed they heard one of the ponies whinny, and Uncle Arthur's voice in the yard as he talked to them.

"Do you think we might be able to go to the theatre with them one day?" Angela asked Ian, as they went down the stairs.

"We can ask Uncle Arthur," replied Ian.

The big wooden clock on the living-room wall pointed to seven o'clock. There was no sign of breakfast, although Bluey was eating seed in his cage, and scattering it over the floor with little shakes of his head.

The children washed in the tiny pink and white bathroom which opened off the kitchen, and then hesitated in the doorway.

"Do you think it would be all right if we went outside?" asked Angela.

"I should think so."

Ian opened the back door. Outside, it was just starting to get light, and they could see a few details of the yard. A dustbin stood in a corner at the bottom of the steps, and on the other side was a concrete coal-bunker. Partner was sitting on this, washing his paws, and light shone from the ponies' shed. Inside they could see Uncle Arthur moving about, and Ian led the way down the steps.

"Hello," exclaimed their uncle, as they paused rather uncertainly in the shed doorway. "Early risers, I see. Say 'Good morning,' Magic, Moonshine," he instructed them.

The ponies lifted their heads from their piles of hay, and Magic whinnied.

"Come on, Moonshine," urged Uncle Arthur.

24

Moonshine made a soft wuffling sound in his nostrils, and then turned back to his hay.

"He's not so talkative as Magic," explained their uncle.

He had already sorted the dirty straw out of the ponies' beds, and it lay on a split sack between the two stalls. Uncle Arthur was spreading the clean straw back over the floor in Magic's stall. Moonshine's was finished, and looked neat and comfortable.

"Can I fill the water-buckets?" asked Ian, seeing them empty.

"Oh yes, yes, of course, if you'd like to," agreed Uncle Arthur.

Ian went out with the buckets and Uncle Arthur folded the sack so that all the dirty straw was inside, swung it up on to his back, and carried it round to the side of the shed. The small manure pile there was neatly and carefully covered with sacking.

Partner strolled in, and jumped up on to Magic's rail to have his head stroked by Angela. Ian came staggering back with the buckets, slopping water over his shoes.

Both he and Angela had decided to wear jeans, so that it would not matter if they got dirty.

"Well, that's all," announced Uncle Arthur, a few minutes later. The stable was clean and tidy, both buckets stood, full, in position, and Magic and Moonshine were eating hay with comfortable munching sounds. "Time for our breakfast now. Do you both eat boiled eggs?"

"Oh yes," Angela assured him, as they walked across the yard.

In the house Uncle Arthur exclaimed with surprise at seeing that it was ten past eight.

"Must open the shop," he told them. "Back in a minute."

He hurried through the green-curtained door, and they heard him unbolting the outside door. Someone came in at once, and they heard voices and the clang of the till. Uncle Arthur just had time to come out and put the saucepan on to boil for the eggs before another customer came into the shop.

"Shall I set the table?" Angela asked, as

he hurried towards the shop door.

"Oh, yes, certainly. Be a great help," agreed Uncle Arthur.

Angela and Ian set the table, hunting in drawers and cupboards for the cloth and the cutlery. They found the plates and cups on the plastic draining rack in the kitchen. The saucepan was boiling by now, but Uncle Arthur was still in the shop. Angela decided to put the eggs in herself. She found the box of eggs and a large spoon and lowered three carefully into the water. Then she looked at the living-room clock and carefully began to time four minutes. Ian cut bread, and put it under the grill to toast, and filled and switched on the electric kettle. Uncle Arthur came back to find everything ready.

The eggs were done perfectly. Angela felt very proud of them as she dipped her spoon into her own, and Uncle Arthur congratulated her on them.

"I'm not very good at eggs," he told them. "Always get them too hard or too runny.

I'll have to leave them to you."

"I like cooking," Angela told him eagerly. "I've done a little bit, when Aunt Mavis had time to let me. I'd like to do some."

"Oh well," Uncle Arthur looked rather worried. "I suppose you could. Mustn't burn yourself, though. Your Aunt Mavis would be after me if I let you hurt yourselves."

"I'll be very careful," Angela promised him. Partner came in through his own cat-flap in the kitchen door, and was given milk and half a tin of cat food. Everyone helped to clear away, and Ian offered to do the washing up. Uncle Arthur had to dash away to serve in the shop, and when he came back Ian asked if they would be able to go to the theatre with the ponies one day.

"I don't see why not," replied Uncle Arthur. "Have to ask permission though. I'll do that tonight. Grace, or rather, Miss Lawley, is coming in to stay with you while I'm at the theatre."

"Miss Lawley?" asked Ian. "Is that the lady we saw in the shop yesterday?"

"In the shop? Oh my goodness, no, that was Mrs Pearson, May Pearson, a neighbour," replied Uncle Arthur. "No, Grace is quite different. You'll like Grace; she's a very nice person. Very nice indeed. Not that Mrs Pearson isn't nice, of course, but still Grace is different."

Ian and Angela thoroughly enjoyed their first day at Uncle Arthur's. After the washing up was done and the beds made Uncle Arthur's assistant, Mrs Randall, arrived to take over the shop for two hours while he took the ponies out for their exercise.

"Can't leave them shut up all day," he explained. "It wouldn't do them any good. It's not natural to keep any animal shut up all the time. They need exercise and fresh air just like we do."

Before going out Magic and Moonshine had to be groomed. First Uncle Arthur brushed them over with a stiff, yellow brush called a dandy brush. This removed all the bits of straw and stains from their coats. Then he picked up a softer, flat brush and a flat metal comb with a lot of teeth and began to rub the brush over Moonshine. After each stroke he cleaned the brush by pulling it over the comb, and every few minutes he tapped the comb on the floor to knock out the grease.

"Could we try, do you think?" Ian asked, when he and Angela had been watching for a bit.

"Yes, of course you can, why not?" asked Uncle Arthur. "Ladies first."

He handed the brush and comb to Angela, and she tried to imitate the way that he had used them. It was much harder work than it looked, however, and she did not seem to be getting very much dirt out of the ponies' thick coats. Ian tried, but he was not much more successful. Uncle Arthur assured them that they would soon learn, and gave Magic a quick brush over.

"They've got their winter coats at present," he told the children. "It's easier in summer, when they've got less hair."

He went to fetch the ponies' bridles from

the back of the shed, and Ian and Angela watched him slip the metal bits into their mouths and the leather straps over their ears. Magic and Moonshine followed him eagerly out of their stalls and into the yard.

Uncle Arthur was much too big to ride the ponies, of course, and even Ian and Angela would have been rather big, and so the ponies were led. There were white webbing leading reins clipped to their bits, and Uncle Arthur led them one on either side of him. Ian opened the yard gate, and they all went out on to the cinder path which ran between the back yards of the two rows of houses.

Ian and Angela soon discovered that Uncle Arthur and his ponies were very well known in the district. A lot of people waved or spoke to them when they came out into the quiet street at the end of the path, and children came running to pat the ponies.

Magic and Moonshine seemed to enjoy all the attention. They pricked their ears and arched their necks to enjoy the patting and "asked" by lifting one forefoot and waving it in the air. Their feet made a soft thudding sound as they walked, and Angela remembered that most horses and ponies clattered on the roads.

"Don't they wear iron shoes?" she asked Uncle Arthur.

"Oh no. Not for the stage," replied Uncle Arthur. "They do in the summer, when they go to fêtes and horse shows and things. For the stage they wear rubber shoes. Rubber doesn't slip."

"Don't they go on the stage at all in summer?" asked Ian.

"Oh, sometimes, sometimes," said Uncle Arthur. "I have them shod specially then."

Their walk took them round a lot of quiet little streets, through a square with a rather overgrown garden in the centre, and over a canal bridge on to a big recreation ground.

"Like to lead one?" Uncle Arthur asked Ian.

"Please," agreed Ian.

Uncle Arthur handed him Moonshine's

leading rein, and Angela felt very envious. Perhaps her turn would come in a few minutes.

"I'll just give Magic his run," said Uncle Arthur.

He let Magic's long leading rein out to its full length, and the little pony began to circle round him, breaking into a quick, gay trot. Moonshine shook his head, and put his nose down to smell the damp, trampled winter grass.

The recreation ground was very quiet. It was a dull, slightly misty morning. The only other people there were a man in a blue track-suit, running slowly round the football ground, and a woman with a small dog. The woman waved to Uncle Arthur, who waved back, and Angela and Ian realized that here, too, the ponies were a familiar sight.

After about ten minutes Uncle Arthur stopped Magic, and handed him to Angela to hold while Moonshine had his run. When the bigger pony had had his turn Uncle Arthur brought him back, and stood just in

33

front of Magic with his back to the pony.

"Good boy, Moonshine," he said.

He patted the pony's neck, ignoring Magic, who pricked his ears and then took a step forward. Reaching out his nose, he nudged his master in the back.

"What? Who did that?" exclaimed Uncle Arthur, looking round.

Magic pricked his ears, and gazed innocently into the distance.

"Was that you?" Uncle Arthur demanded, looking severely at a startled Angela.

"No, it was ..." began Angela, but Uncle Arthur quickly turned away again.

Doubtfully Angela looked at Ian. Was Uncle Arthur cross about something? But Ian was grinning, and looking back at their uncle Angela saw him wink. Suddenly she understood. This was part of Magic and Moonshine's act.

Again Magic nudged Uncle Arthur, and again he turned round to see nothing but an innocent pony looking away across the big, misty field.

"Did you see anyone? Who was it?" he asked the children.

"I didn't see anything," said Ian. "Did you, Angela?"

"No," agreed Angela. "I didn't see anything either."

"Funny," said Uncle Arthur. He turned back to Moonshine. "Did you see anything?" he asked the pony.

Moonshine shook his head vigorously. Magic went up closer to Uncle Arthur, and gave him a harder push. This time he went on pushing when Uncle Arthur turned round, and his master put his hands on his hips and nodded.

"So it was you, was it?" he said. "I suppose you want some attention as well?"

Magic nodded his head, and Uncle Arthur put his hand in his pocket and brought out a slice of carrot. Moonshine immediately

36

nudged him as well, and Uncle Arthur brought out a second slice for him.

"Clever, aren't they?" he asked the children, while Magic and Moonshine munched. "Magic does that routine with Donnie Shaw in the show."

"Does he do it all on his own?" asked Angela.

"I give him signals," replied Uncle Arthur. "Had to teach Donnie the same ones, of course, and get them working together. Now watch."

He turned his back on Magic again, and patted Moonshine. This time, watching closely, the children saw that he also quickly put one hand behind his back as he turned. Magic pricked his ears, and immediately went to nudge Uncle Arthur again. This time he got his slice of carrot at once.

"Always give a reward," explained Uncle Arthur. "Rewards, not punishments. That's how to train animals."

"Is there a signal for everything?" asked Ian.

"Yes. A signal or a word," replied his uncle. "Watch."

Angela and Ian watched carefully as Uncle Arthur turned to Moonshine.

"Do you like sugar?" he asked, holding one hand in front of him. He moved it up and down slightly, and Moonshine nodded his head.

"Do you like vinegar?" asked Uncle Arthur. This time he moved his hand sideways, and Moonshine shook his head.

"Do you see?" he asked the children.

Ian and Angela said that they did.

"Why don't you carry a long stick with them?" asked Ian. "In circuses the people with horses always do. Don't they give them signals with that?"

"Yes, in circus," agreed Uncle Arthur. "But it wouldn't look right in our kind of act, would it? It's a bit harder this way, but it looks a lot better, I think." He looked at his watch, and then began to gather up Magic and Moonshine's reins. "My goodness," he exclaimed. "Ten to twelve. Must get back. Mrs Randall has to cook her husband's dinner by one o'clock. Come along."

Ian was allowed to lead Moonshine for part of the way, and Uncle Arthur let Angela lead Magic up the cinder path to their gate.

"Which is the cleverest?" asked Angela, as they watched Uncle Arthur give the ponies their mid-day feeds. These consisted of half buckets of greenish-brown cubes, which looked rather like thick, chopped up bits of stick.

"Oh dear, not in front of them," exclaimed Uncle Arthur. "One of them might be hurt."

Angela stared at Magic and Moonshine.

"Can they really understand that much?" she asked.

"You never know," replied Uncle Arthur. "Mustn't risk it. Might have one of them going on strike."

As they went across the yard he said, "Cleverest? Well, I don't know. Moonshine's very reliable, never gets excited. I can leave him standing on his own in the middle

39

of the ring at a show. He won't move until he's told. But Magic—he's the quick one. He learns quickly, and he's got a sense of humour. Loves to get the laughs. He's a real showman, in fact."

"Which do you like the best?" asked Ian.

"Now, you mustn't ask that," Uncle Arthur told him. "Never have a favourite. They might know, you see. Now, I must go and let poor Mrs Randall get home."

He hurried through into the shop, and Angela and Ian looked at one another.

"I bet he has got a favourite," said Ian.

"Yes—Magic," said Angela, and they laughed.

3 · Grace

For lunch they had chops, frozen peas, and potatoes, all rather over-cooked, and followed by cold apple pie and some ice cream from the shop fridge. The apple pie was delicious.

"Grace made it," explained Uncle Arthur, when Angela said how nice it was. "Cooking's one of her hobbies. She said you'd probably starve if you had to live entirely on my cooking, and so she made a few things to help out."

It began to rain after lunch, and so the children stayed in the house. There were some games in one of the drawers in Uncle Arthur's big dresser, and they played Snap, draughts, dominoes, and Snakes and Ladders. Uncle Arthur joined in when there was no one in the shop, but the bell was busy

41

for most of the afternoon.

People came in for a packet of cigarettes, a bar of chocolate, a magazine, or to change a book at the little lending library. This filled three shelves in one corner of the shop.

Uncle Arthur let the children go into the shop with him, and they both found it very strange to be on the wrong side of the counter. Angela was allowed to work the till, and Ian scrambled up and down the ladder to fetch things from the higher shelves.

At half-past four Angela made some tea and put out cake and biscuits which they ate in a short lull from the bell. The shop was supposed to close at half-past six, but it was ten to seven before it was empty long enough for Uncle Arthur to lock the door and pull down the blind.

"Have to hurry now," he told them. "Must be at the theatre by a quarter to eight."

There was tinned meat and tomatoes for supper, with bread and butter and the cherry cake to follow. Uncle Arthur ate his very fast, and Ian and Angela were still eating their meat when he said that he must fetch the van round.

"Do the ponies go in a van, then?" asked Ian, who had supposed that Magic and Moonshine walked to the theatre.

"Oh my goodness, yes," replied Uncle Arthur. "Can't have them walking there, especially on a wet night. I'd never get them looking clean again. Have to groom them again at the theatre anyway. Besides, I don't like having them out on the roads after dark. Not safe; there's too much traffic."

"Can we watch them go into the van?" asked Angela, and their uncle said that they could.

Uncle Arthur backed his van up the cinder path to the back gate, and Angela and Ian went out in their mackintoshes to watch. The van was very gay. In the light of a nearby street lamp they could see the red, green, and yellow paintwork. The mudguards were red, the bodywork green, and the doors yellow, and big yellow letters along both

43

sides read "Magic and Moonshine". In smaller letters beneath the names was written "Wonder ponies of stage and screen".

"Have they been in films?" Ian asked Uncle Arthur, when he had read this.

"Well, they once made a commercial for television, advertising shampoo," replied Uncle Arthur. "That's the screen, isn't it?"

Ian agreed that it certainly was.

The shape of the van was rather tall and narrow, and the original back doors had been changed to a ramp for the ponies to walk up. Inside it was divided into two halves by a padded partition, and the sides were also padded. A padded bar went across in front of the ponies, very low down as they were so small. Beyond this there was a space for equipment to be stored.

Magic and Moonshine had heard the van arrive, and they were waiting eagerly in their stalls. Magic especially looked excited: his little creamy ears were pricked, and his dark eyes shone. Moonshine looked interested, but calmer.

Uncle Arthur led Magic into the van first, while Ian held Moonshine. Both ponies went in happily, without any hesitation, and certainly the van looked comfortable with its bed of straw on the wooden floor. A net filled with hay hung in front of each pony, for them to eat on the journey. A little light in the roof made it easy for Uncle Arthur to see to tie the ponies up.

Uncle Arthur had got out, and come round to raise the ramp when a voice behind the children said, "Hello. I'm just in time, then."

"Hello, Grace," exclaimed Uncle Arthur, turning to beam at her. "Meet Angela and Ian. This is Miss Lawley," he told them.

Ian and Angela turned to see a nice-looking, dark-haired woman in a green mackintosh smiling at them. She looked younger than Uncle Arthur, and her dark eyes were warm and friendly.

"Just Grace, please," she said. "I see you've become fans already. When is Arthur taking you to watch them on the stage?"

"I'm going to ask Mr Woodward about

it tonight," Uncle Arthur told her. "If he agrees, they can come backstage with us."

"I'm sure he will," said Grace. "Aren't you going to be late, Arthur? It's twenty-five to."

"Is it? I must be off," exclaimed Uncle Arthur. "See you later. Goodbye, all. Look after Grace, won't you, kids?"

"Goodbye," said Angela and Ian, and Grace waved. Uncle Arthur got into the cab, and the van moved slowly away down the path.

"Come on," said Grace. "Let's go into the dry."

The yard seemed suddenly empty without Magic and Moonshine moving and snorting in their shed. Partner was waiting on the top step to precede them into the house.

"You'd better finish your tea," Grace told them, when they had taken off their wet mackintoshes. "Trust Arthur to be in such a hurry you didn't have time before he went."

She laughed, felt the tea pot, and put the kettle on to boil for more. Then she sat down at the table with them, and asked them how they liked it at Uncle Arthur's.

Ian and Angela found Grace very easy to talk to. She was not shy with them, as Uncle Arthur had been at first and still was a bit. Nor was she stiff, like Aunt Mavis, and she seemed really interested in them. Soon Angela especially felt that if Grace was really their aunt she would be happy to stay with her for always. She felt much the same about Uncle Arthur, but living with him might be rather a responsibility.

When they had finished tea Grace sat down at the piano and asked them if they liked music.

"Well . . ." said Ian doubtfully, trying to be polite. "We do sometimes."

Grace laughed. "I mean songs, and things like that," she said.

"I like singing at school," said Angela.

"Do you know this?" Grace began to play, and Angela recognised *Bobby Shafto*. Soon they were all singing. Grace knew dozens of songs and tunes. She played old ones like *Mollie Malone* and *The Grey Goose*, songs from musicals such as *Oklahoma* and *Mary Poppins*, slow traditional ones like *Greensleeves* and *Over the Sea to Skye* and jazzy ones like *Yellow Submarine*.

Angela and Ian hummed the ones that they did not know the words to, and the time flashed past. They had never realized how much fun a piano could be. Aunt Mavis had one, a polished beauty that stood in her front room. It was very different from this battered instrument of Uncle Arthur's, and they were strictly forbidden to touch it. It was certainly not considered a thing to have fun with.

"Do you play the piano a lot?" Ian asked Grace, when they finally paused for breath.

"Yes, I'm a piano teacher," explained Grace. "And I play for dancing classes at a school twice a week. Then there are Arthur's film shows. I play for those as well. That's a lot of fun."

"Film shows?" inquired Angela, puzzled.

"Yes. He's got a projector, and he shows old silent films sometimes, in here," replied Grace. "All the neighbours come, and we

48

have quite a party. I play the piano to accompany the films. Cinemas always had a pianist before films had sound."

She played a few deep, sinister notes on the piano.

"That's the villain's music," she explained. She played a pretty, tinkling tune. "That's for the heroine."

Some fast, exciting music like horses galloping was for the chase, and there was a slow, sad piece of music for when things went wrong.

"Do you have to watch the film, and make the music fit in, then?" asked Ian.

"Yes. And you mustn't get left behind," replied Grace. "The wrong bit of music at a dramatic moment could ruin everything."

It was getting late by now, and Grace said that it was time they went to bed. She got out milk and biscuits, and said that she would come up to look at them after they were in bed.

"Isn't she nice?" whispered Angela, as they went up the stairs. "It is fun here. I hope Aunt Mavis won't come home too quickly."

"So do I," agreed Ian. "It'll seem awfully dull back in Surbiton."

Next morning Uncle Arthur asked them if they had enjoyed themselves with Grace. Ian and Angela told him that they had.

"Thought you would," said Uncle Arthur. "Couldn't help liking Grace, could you? I've often thought I ought to marry her. Don't suppose she'd have me, though." He laughed, and got up to answer the shop bell. Angela and Ian looked at each other.

"I wish Uncle Arthur would marry Grace," said Angela. "Perhaps we might be able to stay here, then, if she was here to look after us."

"It would be terrific if we could," agreed Ian. "But he might only have been joking."

Angela was afraid that he might be right. It was a nice thing to dream about, however. Living with Uncle Arthur and Grace would be much nicer than living with Aunt Mavis.

"By the way," said Uncle Arthur, when they were washing up, "I asked about you two coming to the show. It's all right, so you can come along and see the performance tonight. Backstage, of course. I'll fix you up with seats out front another night."

"Oh, thank you," cried Angela, and Ian said, "Gosh, how marvellous. Thank you."

They grinned at each other in excited delight. It had been fun at home with Grace, but how much more exciting it would be to see Magic and Moonshine on the stage, and to be with them backstage as though they too were part of the show.

The second day at Uncle Arthur's passed as quickly and as interestingly as the first. Mrs Randall came to look after the shop again while Uncle Arthur and the children took Magic and Moonshine for their walk.

In the afternoon Angela and Ian went to do some shopping at the other shops in the street. The other shopkeepers knew who they were, and all about them, and were very friendly. It was as though they really be-

51

longed, thought Angela, as they walked back to their uncle's.

It was very exciting that evening to watch Magic and Moonshine climb the ramp into their van, and to know that tonight they were going as well. Grace had called round to see what was happening, and she was there to wave them off.

There was plenty of room in the cab beside Uncle Arthur, and the children discovered a little window behind them through which they could see into the back. Uncle Arthur had a switch in the cab which turned on the inside light over the ponies, so that he could see them whenever he wished.

It was not far from Uncle Arthur's to the theatre, and Ian and Angela thoroughly enjoyed the ride. They were soon in a much busier, more brightly lighted district than the one in which Uncle Arthur lived. From the high cab they had a good view of the traffic and the lighted shop windows.

It was a cold evening, and everyone seemed to be hurrying along the pavements with their coat collars turned up, but a lot of people glanced at the van, and paused to stare at its gay paint, and to read the words painted on the side.

The theatre stood half-way along a wide road of shops, its glass doors open to the warmly lighted foyer. A big sign across the front read, "The Corry Empire presents *Cinderella*, a grand pantomime spectacular, starring Donnie Shaw."

"It doesn't say anything about Magic and Moonshine," exclaimed Angela, disappointed.

"Not up there. We're not stars yet," replied Uncle Arthur. "But they've got their names on the other posters, the ones by the doors."

To Angela and Ian's surprise he did not stop outside the theatre, but drove straight past.

"Got to go round to the stage door," he explained, seeing them exchange glances. "First turn on the left."

The van turned, and a few minutes later they entered a dimly lighted yard, behind

53

the massive back of the Corry Empire. Uncle Arthur parked the van beside a row of cars, switched off the engine, and opened the cab door. In the back one of the ponies whinnied, and Uncle Arthur said, "That's Magic. He knows we've arrived."

The ponies came out of the van as eagerly as they had gone in. Ian was trusted to lead Moonshine across the yard, and Uncle Arthur handed Angela one of the hay nets to carry. There was a huge pair of iron doors set in the wall of the theatre, with a dim light beside them. Uncle Arthur explained that the big pieces of scenery were taken in that way. Their way in was through a smaller door set into the large ones. Magic went through first, lifting his feet neatly over the step, and Moonshine followed. Angela closed the little door behind them, and they were backstage at the Corry Empire.

4 · Backstage

The door opened into a long, wide corridor, stone-floored, and with whitewashed brick walls. Uncle Arthur turned right, and a little further on they came to another pair of doors. Beyond these lay what really seemed to be another world.

Backstage, the children soon discovered, was a confusing place. Tall pieces of canvas and wood, the scenery "flats", and the huge canvas "back-cloths" on which were painted the background to each scene, hid the stage from view. Ropes and pulleys dangled from the high, shadowy roof, and the lighting was dim and dusty.

One big, dark opening led to the scenery store room, and through a gap between the "flats" the children caught a glimpse of the stage. The red curtains were down, hiding the audience, and there were gay market stalls in position, ready for the opening scene.

There were a lot of people hurrying about behind the stage : men in jeans and sweaters carrying stage properties and bits of scenery, and other people in strange costumes and thick make-up. Most of them spoke to Uncle Arthur, and patted the ponies, and one thin, pretty girl wearing a red skirt with big patches and a white, loose-sleeved blouse gave Magic an apple core.

"Was that Cinderella?" asked Angela, when the girl had gone.

"No. That was Julie. She's a dancer in the chorus," replied Uncle Arthur.

He was making his way right round the back of the stage, and the ponies seemed to know where they were going.

"They've got their own corner, you know," said Uncle Arthur. "Just round here."

Magic and Moonshine's corner was an empty alcove which Uncle Arthur said was sometimes used for storing extra scenery.

There was sand on the board floor to prevent them from slipping, and to soak up any moisture, and two rings were fixed to the wall. Magic and Moonshine were fastened to these, and Uncle Arthur took the hay net from Angela and tied it between them. He filled an empty bucket with water, and the ponies were settled.

"When do they go on?" asked Ian.

"Magic does his bit with Donnie Shaw just before the interval," replied Uncle Arthur. "The transformation scene, where they pull Cinderella's coach to the ball, is near the end."

Angela remembered the story, and how the rats and the pumpkin were supposed to turn into the ponies and the coach. She could not imagine how it would be done.

"Are there really rats?" she asked. "To turn into ponies?"

"Oh yes, there are rats all right," Uncle Arthur told her. "You'll see. It's all done with the lights—lights and a gauze curtain. Very clever."

It sounded impossible to Angela, but she supposed that they would see what happened later on.

"Hello, Arthur," said a tall man with a beard. "Got your helpers with you, I see."

"That's right, Frank," agreed Uncle Arthur. "Angela and Ian. Couldn't manage without them."

"No. Need someone to help you to hold those fire-eaters down," said Frank, smiling. "If you want to watch later on," he told the children, "you can stand over there." He pointed to the right hand side of the stage. "Behind the prompter. But stand well back and keep quiet, won't you?"

Angela and Ian promised him that they would, and Frank went off.

"Stage manager," explained Uncle Arthur. "Nice fellow, Frank."

"What is a prompter?" inquired Ian.

"The person who reads the lines to himself as the performers act on the stage, and tells them what comes next if they forget," replied their uncle.

A bell rang somewhere, and he said, "Five minutes to go."

Moonshine was eating hay calmly, his ears relaxed and his eyes half closed. Magic, however, was trying to look round, his ears sharply pricked and his eyes bright. He did not seem interested in his hay, and as the space behind the stage began to fill up with people in gay costumes he began to paw the floor with one small front hoof. Uncle Arthur went to stand beside the pony, putting one arm round his neck, and talking to him softly. Magic grew a little quieter, and Frank said, "Everyone on stage, please. Opening number."

Most of the gaily dressed girls and men went on to the stage, and from beyond the curtain Angela and Ian heard the exciting sound of the orchestra tuning up.

"Quiet, please," warned Frank, and the instruments were suddenly playing a merry, dancing tune. There was a swish and a rattle as the curtain went back, and the children jumped as the chorus began to sing only a

59

few feet away from them, beyond the scenery.

"Why not go and watch?" whispered Uncle Arthur. "I'll warn you when it's time to get Magic ready."

Angela and Ian nodded, and crept round to stand where Frank had suggested. The prompter was a girl with long, dark hair, dressed in slacks and a sweater. She was sitting on a low canvas stool, a typewritten script on her knee, reading the words silently and intently as the people on the stage spoke them. It was easy for the children to see over her head, and they found that they had a good view of most of the stage.

The pantomime at the Corry Empire was not really a very big one, but to Angela and Ian, watching from their dark corner, the warm, bright stage seemed enchanted. People in costume stood in the dusty wings, waiting to go on, just seeming ordinary in spite of their make-up and fancy dress. Then they stepped out into the light and colour, and suddenly they were people from a fairy story. The change was dazzling and confusing, and the nearness of the music and singing made the children feel almost part of it themselves.

There was not a big audience, but there were enough people in the seats to fill the theatre with laughter and clapping, and this helped to give the show life. Angela and Ian had almost forgotten the ponies when Julie, from the chorus, touched Ian on the shoulder and said that Uncle Arthur was getting Magic ready.

It did not take much work to get Magic ready for his first appearance with Donnie Shaw. Uncle Arthur was polishing his creamy coat with a soft body-brush, and Ian and Angela were allowed to brush out his silvery mane and tail. Then Uncle Arthur unfastened his rope, and led him round to the opposite side of the stage from the prompter, ready for his entrance.

Magic knew that it was time for his special bit. His eyes shone, and he arched his neck against the pull of the rope. The scene was in the forest, and the back-cloth was painted with green trees, yellow and blue flowers, and red toadstools. The canvas "flats" were shaped and painted like trees. Donnie Shaw, as Buttons, was helping Cinderella to gather sticks. Cinderella wandered off the stage, still searching, and Donnie stood looking at the big pile that they had collected, wondering how to carry them.

"Oh dear," he said. "I shall never be able to manage all those on my own. I wish I had someone to help me."

This was Magic's cue, the moment when he had to go on to the stage. Donnie clasped both hands behind his back, and Uncle Arthur unbuckled Magic's head collar. Completely loose, Magic trotted on to the stage. He went straight up behind Donnie, or Buttons, and pushed him in the back.

"Here, who did that?" exclaimed Buttons, turning round.

As he had done on the recreation ground with Uncle Arthur, Magic stared innocently into the distance.

"Was it you?" Buttons asked him. He was holding his hand out, and he moved it sideways slightly. Magic shook his head. Buttons turned his back again, and once more Magic gave him a push, and then looked innocent.

The audience was starting to laugh now, and Buttons turned away again. Once more Magic pushed him, and this time he went on pushing with his nose when Buttons turned back. Buttons shook his fist at the pony, and Magic jumped sideways and trotted off. Buttons chased him round the stage, in and out of the "trees", until, at another signal from Buttons, Magic swung round and began to do the chasing himself.

The audience roared, and Angela glanced at Uncle Arthur. He was watching his pony carefully, and proudly. Angela thought that he was right to be proud, after training a pony like Magic.

At last Magic stopped chasing Buttons, and they stood and looked at one another.

"Look," said Buttons. "Why don't we make friends? You carry my sticks, and I'll introduce you to the most beautiful girl in the world."

Magic shook his head, and then lifted his nose and curled back his top lip.

"Oh, so you don't think much of that?" asked Buttons. "Well then, suppose I tell you about the dancing classes everyone is going to, ready for the Prince's ball?"

Again Magic shook his head.

"I bet you can't dance, anyway," retorted Buttons.

The orchestra struck up a rumba, and Buttons dropped his hand to his side, moving so that he could touch Magic's flank. Magic pricked his ears, and as Buttons began to dance a rumba the pony began to swing his hind quarters from side to side as though he, too, was dancing. The tune changed to a waltz, and Magic and Buttons circled the stage, twirling round in circles to the music.

The fairy story enchantment of the stage worked on Magic as well, and Angela found it easy to imagine that he really was a fairy pony, part of the mysterious forest, and not one of Uncle Arthur's pantomime ponies at all. The soft, warm lighting darkened the colour of his creamy coat, and his silver tail swirled behind him, shot with red, blue, and green from the footlights.

Then the waltz came to an end, and Magic and Buttons faced the audience in a low bow, Buttons with right foot extended, Magic

down on his right knee with his other leg stretched in front of him.

"I know," said Buttons, when they were on their feet again. "If you carry my sticks, I'll give you a bag of carrots."

Magic nodded vigorously, and went to stand beside the pile of sticks. Buttons swung the bundle on to the pony's back, and Magic followed him off the stage to where Uncle Arthur was waiting.

The applause for Magic was long and loud, and Uncle Arthur fed him on carrots while Ian and Angela patted him.

"He's wonderful," Angela told her uncle, and Ian agreed. Uncle Arthur's face was red with pleasure as they praised the pony, and Magic looked smug as he buried his nose in his hay. Now that his first, and most exciting, appearance was over he was as ready to eat as Moonshine was.

It took much longer to get the ponies ready for their appearance with the coach in the transformation scene. Both Magic and Moonshine's manes and tails were plaited,

66

and the plaits were threaded with ribbon. They wore tall ostrich feathers, coloured silver and blue, on the headbands of their bridles, and the bridles and their harness were also silver and blue. The leather was studded with shiny things that looked like rubies and diamonds, although Uncle Arthur said that they were made of glass.

When the ponies were plaited and harnessed they had to be fastened to the coach. Cinderella's coach was made of wood, and the framework was set on big wheels. There was a single narrow seat inside, and the roof was arched. As it was supposed to be made of glass there was no covering over the wooden struts, and Uncle Arthur said that Cinderella and her attendants had to remember not to put their hands between them.

"Give the show away if they did," he said. "You can't put your hand through glass."

The coach was painted silver, and the woodwork was set with gold and silver sequins and more bits of coloured glass. It looked so light and fragile that it did not seem possible that anyone could really ride in it.

The coach was already in position at the back of the stage when Uncle Arthur led the ponies out to harness them. The second, or drop curtain, was down, hiding the comedians who were making the audience laugh at the front of the stage.

Between the ponies and coach and the main part of the stage there was a thin curtain made of gauze. Uncle Arthur said that while the lights shone on it from the front the audience could not see through. It was when those lights went out, and the ones at the back came on, that the ponies and coach would be seen.

This seemed incredible to Ian and Angela, for when the drop curtain went up they could see the stage, with its set of kitchen fireplace and cupboards, and the table with the cage of white rats and the pumpkin, quite clearly. They could also see the audience, and it was hard to believe that they themselves could not be seen at all.

Uncle Arthur and the children waited with the ponies while on the stage Cinderella's fairy godmother appeared, and granted her wish to go to the ball. Magic and Moonshine stood very quietly, seeming to understand that they must not make any noise. Then all the lights went down, and part of the chorus danced a fairy ballet. They wore luminous frocks, and shone blue, green, and red in the dark.

Then Cinderella came quietly back on to the stage, and two members of the chorus came to take the ponies from Uncle Arthur. He hurried the children off the stage, and the lights came up behind the gauze curtain. The audience gasped, and then began to clap as the ponies and their lovely little coach became visible, and as they saw Cinderella in her beautiful ball gown. Then the gauze curtain rose, and Cinderella stepped carefully into her coach. Led by two members of the chorus the ponies drew Cinderella's coach away, off the stage, to the ball.

"So that's how it's done," exclaimed Ian.

"I've always wondered."

Uncle Arthur laughed as he began to un-harness the two ponies. "Not very magical really," he said. "But clever. Very clever."

The pantomime was almost over. Cinderella met the prince, lost her slipper on the stairs at midnight, and was found again in rags by her kitchen fire. The entire cast, including Magic and Moonshine, went on to the stage for the finale, which took place at Cinderella's wedding to the Prince. Then the curtain came down for the last time.

Angela and Ian helped Uncle Arthur to make sure that all the harness and trappings were safely back in their box, then they were ready to go home. Uncle Arthur and Ian led the ponies back along the corridor, and Angela followed them out into the damp and chilly yard.

It felt very cold outside after the warmth inside the theatre. The children were shivering as they watched Uncle Arthur load the ponies, and the thought of the living-room fire and of bed was very inviting. They could not remember ever having been out so late before.

The streets were very dark and quiet as they drove home, and there was hardly anyone about. It was very welcome to enter the yard at Uncle Arthur's and see the kitchen light shining, and the back door open. Grace had waited for them to come home. She had everything ready for hot chocolate drinks, and the cake tin was on the table. Partner lay stretched out luxuriously in front of the glowing fire, and Bluey was dozing with his head under his wing.

Angela was almost too sleepy to eat her cake, although Ian was still wide awake, and asking eager questions about things they had seen at the theatre. Angela hardly remembered Grace taking her upstairs, and tucking her into bed, but there was something very comfortable about it all.

5 · A new trick

For the first time since they had come to Uncle Arthur's Angela did not wake up when the paper boys arrived in the morning. Ian woke her in the end.

"It's half-past nine," he told her, as she sat up, rubbing her eyes. "We had breakfast ages ago. We left you some bacon and toast, but I expect it'll be pretty hard by now. Oh, and there's a letter from Aunt Mavis."

"A letter?" Angela was wide awake at once. "She doesn't want us back yet, does she?"

"Oh no, not yet," Ian assured her. "But she says she hopes she won't have to be away too long. She says her mother's leg isn't very bad, and she'll be able to get about again in two or three weeks. She doesn't want us to put upon Uncle Arthur for any longer than we must."

"But we aren't 'putting upon him', are we?" asked Angela anxiously. "He seems to like having us here, now he's getting used to us."

"I think he does like it," agreed Ian. "But Aunt Mavis doesn't know that."

"Oh, Ian, I don't want to go back," wailed Angela. "We're always moving about. When we do go back to Aunt Mavis's we'll be sent to stay with someone else again when she has to go away the next time."

"Perhaps we'll come back here next time as well, if Uncle Arthur does enjoy having us," said Ian hopefully. He did not like thinking about going back to Aunt Mavis's neat, tidy, silent flat either, but he supposed that it was unavoidable. But it was no use starting to be miserable about going back yet. They had hardly been with Uncle Arthur for any time at all, and there was no sense in spoiling their stay by thinking about Aunt Mavis's all the time.

By the end of their first week Angela and Ian really began to feel as though they had always lived at Uncle Arthur's. The whistle of the early paper boys and the clang of the shop bell were familiar sounds, and so was Bluey's chatter above their heads as they had breakfast.

They went to the theatre again, to sit in front this time, and applaud with the rest of the audience when Magic did his act. On Sunday they went to church with Grace in the morning, while Uncle Arthur looked after the shop.

In the evening Grace came to tea, and afterwards they all sang round the piano. Then Uncle Arthur set up his projector and showed some short, silent, slap-stick comedies. Grace played the piano while Charlie Chaplin, Little Titch, and Buster Keaton went through their antics, and Angela and Ian laughed until they were helpless.

After Grace had gone home the children went out into the frosty night to help Uncle Arthur to settle the ponies. It did not seem possible that only a week ago they had not known the yard, and the ponies' shed, and Magic and Moonshine drowsing or eating inside. It seemed even less possible that they had not known Grace or Uncle Arthur, and even to Ian it was their old life with Aunt Mavis which began to seem less and less real.

Although it was Uncle Arthur who was supposed to be in charge of them it was Grace who did a lot of the jobs that were too hard for Angela. She took all the washing home with her, saying that it was easy, as she had a washing machine. She also did the more difficult mending. Angela could sew on buttons, and she quite enjoyed doing it, but mending a long tear in Ian's jacket was harder, and Grace did that. She did not come every day, as sometimes she had music lessons to give in the evenings as well as during the day, but usually she called in at some time to make sure that all was well, and that they did not need anything. Uncle Arthur said that he did not know how he would manage without her.

Wednesday was early closing day, and that week Uncle Arthur said that he intended to teach Magic a new trick on Wednesday afternoon. It sounded great fun, and Angela was horrified when she woke up with a sore throat. By lunch time her nose was running, and she was sneezing. Uncle Arthur looked at her anxiously, and awkwardly felt her head.

"Do you often have colds?" he asked her.

"Quite often," Angela told him. "They aren't usually bad. I don't always stay in," she added.

She looked imploringly at Ian, who wished that Grace was there. He suspected that Angela ought to stay in, but it did seem hard on her when Uncle Arthur was going to work with Magic.

"She's not usually ill with colds," he said, after thinking for a moment. It seemed the fairest thing to say.

Uncle Arthur looked relieved. He had no wish to make Angela stay in either.

"That's all right then," he said. "Business

as usual. Now, let's get washed up, and then we can start on old Magic."

"Where will you teach him? Here, or on the recreation ground?" asked Ian.

"Oh, here," replied Uncle Arthur. "They've had their walk for today. Best to train an animal in an enclosed place that it's used to. Nothing to distract it then."

"What are you going to teach him to do?" asked Angela.

"You'll see," Uncle Arthur told her happily. "It isn't anything too hard; he'll have it in half an hour, but it'll dress up."

"Dress up?" Angela was puzzled. She imagined Magic in a hat and ribbons.

"That means it's the sort of trick that can be made to look difficult and exciting," explained Uncle Arthur. "It's simple enough really, like that business of pushing someone, but more can be made of it for the stage."

Angela and Ian understood vaguely. They would soon find out, anyway, when they saw what the trick was going to be.

Uncle Arthur put a head collar on Magic,

and Angela was allowed to lead him out into the yard. Magic knew that something interesting was going to happen, and he looked round with shining eyes. Partner jumped on top of the shed, and settled down as though he were in a ringside seat.

There was an iron rail on either side of the steps up to the back door, and Uncle Arthur took Magic's rope from Angela and tied him to this. He used a simple quick-release knot, leaving a long, loose end. Then he took a carrot out of his pocket, and tied it to the free end. Magic started nosing for it at once, and Uncle Arthur said, "Go on, then. Pull it off."

Magic did so, pulling the carrot free with a quick jerk. The knot, of course, came undone at the same time, and Uncle Arthur made no move to re-fasten it.

"Let him realise he's free first," he explained to the children.

Magic finished his carrot, looked round, and pricked his ears towards his master.

"Come here, then," said Uncle Arthur.

He was standing some distance from the steps, and Magic started towards him at once. Suddenly he seemed to realize that he was free, and he paused, looking back at the steps. Then he walked on to push his nose into Uncle Arthur's hand.

"Let's do that again," said Uncle Arthur, and led Magic back to the steps.

This time Magic seized the carrot at once, and pulled it free. When he had eaten it he paused for a moment and then walked straight across to his master.

"Good boy," Uncle Arthur told him, patting him. "He's getting the idea," he added to Angela and Ian. "It never takes him long to catch on."

By the time they had repeated the same thing six times Magic was grabbing the carrot and walking off loose almost before his master could move away.

"Now," said Uncle Arthur, as he tied Magic up again. "This time we won't use the carrot."

Magic reached out his nose eagerly to the rope, and then stopped in surprise. No carrot.

"Go on," Uncle Arthur encouraged him. "Pull. Here then, Magic. Come on, boy." He held a carrot out towards the pony, and Magic tried to move towards it. Discovering that he was still tied up, he stopped.

"Come on," urged Uncle Arthur. "Pull. Here, Magic."

Magic looked at him, ears pricked, and nostrils wide. Angela and Ian could almost see him thinking. There was no carrot on the rope. There was one in his master's hand, which was held out temptingly, but to get to his master he must get free from the railings. Before, he had found himself free when he had pulled the carrot.

Magic reached out his nose to check again that there was no carrot on the rope. Experimentally he nibbled it with his teeth. Angela almost held her breath. Would Magic realize what he had to do?

Suddenly, Magic decided to try. He seized the rope firmly between his teeth, and gave it a sharp pull. Uncle Arthur had fastened the knot very loosely, and it came free at once. Delighted with himself, Magic kicked up his heels and gave a little squeal before trotting over to get his carrot.

"Good boy. Very good," said Uncle Arthur, patting him hard. He found another carrot in his pocket for the pony. His face glowed with pride in Magic, and Angela and Ian came to praise the pony as well.

They repeated the procedure twice more, and it was obvious that Magic had got the idea.

"Is that the whole trick?" asked Ian. "Or has he got to do anything else?"

"Well, it isn't really the whole trick," replied Uncle Arthur. "But it's enough of it for one day. We'll practise that with him for a bit, and then we'll have Moonshine out as well, and get old Magic untieing him."

"Oh, I see," Ian suddenly understood how the trick would appear. "Magic will sort of rescue Moonshine on the stage."

"That's right, that's it," agreed Uncle Arthur, pleased that they understood. "Good ending to a ring act. I leave Moonshine tied up, pretend to forget him, bow to the audience, and walk off with Magic. Just at the exit we remember. Magic gallops back, unties Moonshine, and they both canter off after me."

"Lovely," exclaimed Angela. "Do you teach him all his tricks like that, with carrots and things?"

"Oh yes. Plenty of encouragement and reward," replied Uncle Arthur. "There are lots of ways of training animals, but that's always been my way. Taught them to bow with carrot. Held it between their front legs, so that they had to bend their necks and knees to get at it. Held it further and further back until I got a bow. After that they soon caught on without the carrot: just a signal with my hand or a stick behind their front legs. Magic, he hardly needs a signal now. Knows when I bow he bows, and that's it. Moonshine still likes to be told."

"What other things can they do?" asked Ian.

"Well, let me see. They can lie down or

sit down, count, open a box, and pick up a handkerchief or take off my hat," listed Uncle Arthur. "And the things you've seen, of course."

"They are clever," said Angela. She sneezed, and pulled out a damp handkerchief to blow her nose. Uncle Arthur looked at her doubtfully and said that they'd better put Magic away and go indoors.

While they were helping Uncle Arthur to settle Magic there was a knock on the yard gate. Ian opened it, and three of Magic and Moonshine's young "fans" came into the yard. Angela and Ian knew them quite well, and had played with them once or twice. Although living with Uncle Arthur had helped them to meet some of the other children, they were not yet really accepted by them.

Magic and Moonshine's fans had been visiting them for a long time, but Uncle Arthur had never trusted them to do more than offer the ponies tit-bits, and sometimes to fill up the water-buckets. But Angela and Ian were allowed to lead them at exercise, and Uncle Arthur had taken them backstage at the theatre with him. The other children had not yet decided whether or not this was quite fair.

"Mum sent some scraps round for them," Jane, who was Ian's age, told Uncle Arthur. She handed him a brown paper carrier bag, and Angela saw that it contained stale bread, cabbage leaves, a few withered carrots, some boiled potatoes, and apple peel. She knew from watching Uncle Arthur before that he would break up the scraps and mix them with Magic and Moonshine's other food.

"My goodness, that is kind of her," Uncle Arthur told Jane. "Coming in to say 'hello' to the lads, are you?"

Jane and her two younger brothers, Simon and Daniel, were allowed to pat Magic and Moonshine and shake hands with them. Ian could not help feeling rather superior when he remembered that they had just helped Uncle Arthur to teach Magic a new trick. He knew that their Uncle did not usually let anyone watch him training the ponies. Angela merely felt rather uncomfortable. She did not like knowing that the others were a bit jealous.

Grace came round while they were having tea. She took one look at Angela's red nose and watery eyes, and said that she hoped Uncle Arthur had kept her in that day. Uncle Arthur went red, mumbled, and looked uncomfortable.

"It isn't very bad, really, Aunt Grace," Angela told her.

"Well, perhaps not. But I do think you'd better stay indoors tomorrow, to give it a chance to go," Grace told her. Angela promised that she would. Staying in was not a very welcome thought, but at the same time it was rather nice to have someone to make a decision like that. It felt comfortable and secure. Angela liked staying with Uncle Arthur, and doing some of the household managing, but it was nice to have Grace about as well.

6 · The pantomime is over

Angela stayed in for two days in the end, as the weather turned very cold. Showers of wet sleet blew over the tall buildings and down the street, and Uncle Arthur gave the ponies extra straw in their beds at night. Partner spread himself out in front of the living-room fire, and hardly moved away from it at all.

Surprisingly Angela enjoyed those two days indoors, although at Aunt Mavis's she would have hated it. Aunt Mavis dreaded them making a noise or a mess, and she would not allow them to use paint or Plasticine in the house. Nor did she like Angela to try her cooking in the shining kitchen except on the few occasions when she had agreed to it as a special treat.

During the holidays the children usually went for a walk in the park every afternoon. In the house they had their rooms to tidy and books to read, and they watched the children's programmes on television. Aunt Mavis never allowed them to watch anything that was later than six o'clock. School, in Surbiton, was a welcome release, but if they stayed here long enough to go to school in the district it would be far less welcome, Angela knew.

There was plenty to do at Uncle Arthur's. Angela spent most of her first morning indoors making jam tarts in the kitchen, while Ian and Uncle Arthur took the ponies out for a short trot round. She cooked chops for lunch. Afterwards Uncle Arthur fetched out a box of photographs of the dog he had owned before the ponies, and of Magic and Moonshine. In between serving in the shop he told them stories that went with the photographs, and he also found some old programmes with the ponies' names in them. Later they got out the games, and had an exciting session of Snap and Snakes and Ladders until tea time.

The second morning was too cold and the sleet was too wet and icy for anyone to go far. Angela was finding paper and pencils to do some drawing when there was a knock on the back door. Opening it she was astonished to find Magic standing on the steps, his hind feet still on the ground, and Uncle Arthur behind him with his mackintosh over his head.

"Open the door wide, Angie," called her uncle. "Go on then, Magic."

Angela pulled the door wide and stood back, and Magic came neatly up the steps and into the kitchen. Uncle Arthur followed, and Ian came running across the wet yard from the shed to join in the fun.

"As you can't come out to talk to him he's come in to see you," explained Uncle Arthur. "Well, Magic, lad? Want some sugar?"

Magic nodded, and his master fetched a bag of brown sugar from a shelf in the kitchen cabinet.

"He's been in here quite often," he told Angela, as the cream-coloured pony licked the thick, dark sugar off his hand. "Not Moonshine, he doesn't like the steps, but Magic's a bit smaller. It's easier for him."

When Magic had finished the sugar he explored the kitchen, reaching up his nose to examine the table and the draining board, and sniffing at the sink. Ian turned the tap on very slowly, and Magic put his nose under the water, and then shook his head. He scattered drops of water over everyone, and Angela giggled. Magic put his nose back under the tap, and reached out his tongue, catching the water on it, and lapping like a cat.

"He's been watching Partner," said Uncle Arthur, laughing. He gave the pony a friendly slap on his round hind quarter. "Well, Magic? Think you're a pussy cat, do you?"

They were still playing with Magic in the kitchen when Grace came through from the shop carrying a basket. She had been doing their shopping for them along with her own.

"Oh, Arthur," she exclaimed. "You and those ponies. I really think you'd give them beds upstairs if you could get them there."

Magic went to meet her with a pleased snuffling noise, but Uncle Arthur looked slightly hurt.

"I don't really think I'm unreasonable with them," he said, rather stiffly.

"No, of course not. I didn't mean it," replied Grace at once.

Uncle Arthur's expression softened, and he smiled. "Oh, I know," he told her. "Just touchy, that's me. Come along, Magic. Time you went out again. Home, boy."

He opened the door, and Magic went down the steps after him and trotted across the yard to his shed. Grace put her basket down on the table, and closed the door.

"How's your cold, Angela?" she asked. "You look a lot better."

The kitchen needed tidying after Magic's visit, and his muddy hoof prints had to be mopped up, but it did not take long. The

91

afternoon was very dark, and at tea time they built up the fire, and toasted crumpets on a long brass toasting fork. On the whole, thought Angela as she lay in bed later, it was almost worth having a cold at Uncle Arthur's.

Angela's cold was much better the next day and she could obviously start to go outside again. This should have made the day very cheerful, but there was a letter from Aunt Mavis at breakfast time which cast a shadow over the morning. In it she said that her mother was recovering quickly now, and she did not expect to be away for more than another week or ten days. The only good thing about this was that it meant there was little point in them starting school. Not that school was so bad. Ian had even found himself missing maths, for he rather liked working with figures. But Angela thought miserably of going back to the rather cold, tidy flat in Surbiton, and even Uncle Arthur seemed unhappy at the idea of them going.

"We shall miss you," he told them. "My

goodness, it will seem quiet. Still, it hasn't happened yet, has it?"

"I wish this was where we always lived," said Angela boldly. "We really do like being here."

"Do you? Do you really?" Uncle Arthur looked pleased. "Glad to hear it. Do you know, I never thought you would. I told Grace you'd think it a pokey place after your aunt's nice flat. She thought I was wrong. Trust Grace to know."

That Saturday was the last night of the pantomime. Angela and Ian had seats in the audience to watch it from, and Grace came as well. Although they had seen it twice before, the children still enjoyed it. Grace had also seen it before, but she laughed and clapped as much as anyone.

At the end the whole cast came on to the stage, including Uncle Arthur with Magic and Moonshine. Bouquets and boxes of chocolates were handed up for Cinderella and Prince Charming, and Uncle Arthur was called forward and given two big bags of carrots for the ponies. Magic and Moonshine bowed in thanks, and then the red curtains swung down for the last time.

"Are you sorry that was the last night?" Angela asked Uncle Arthur, as they drove home. They were all squashed into the cab of the van, with Angela on Grace's knee, and Ian sitting on the gear box between the seats.

"I'm always sorry to see the last of panto-mime for the year," replied Uncle Arthur.

"But there'll be plenty of jobs for us in the spring. Old Magic'll miss it for a bit; he likes to be working, but he'll soon get over it."

On the following Monday morning Mrs Randall did not turn up to take over the shop for the morning. Instead she sent a message round to say that she had 'flu, and could not come.

"Oh dear, oh dear," exclaimed Uncle Arthur. "What about their exercise? Magic's going to be bored anyway, when he finds out there's no pantomime any more."

"Isn't there anyone else who'd look after the shop?" asked Ian.

"No. Grace would, but she's teaching most of the day. The school she plays for has got dancing exams next week too, and so she's doing extra time there this week."

"Uncle Arthur, couldn't we take them for their walk?" asked Angela. "We often lead them, and we know the way you go."

"Yes, we could do it," agreed Ian eagerly.

Uncle Arthur looked doubtful. "They've never been out without me," he said. "I don't know. No, better not. It won't hurt them for a day. We'll let them wander about the yard this morning. It'll give them something to do, anyway. Might try taking them out after dark, though I don't like doing that. It's too easy to get run into round these dark roads."

Magic and Moonshine spent the afternoon wandering about the yard, and seemed to enjoy it. Uncle Arthur decided to try taking them for a short walk after dark, but it was not very successful. Ian walked at the back, carrying a torch covered in red cellophane to warn passing traffic about them, but some of the cars still came uncomfortably close.

"Let's take them home," said Uncle Arthur, after the particularly close passage of a taxi. "I never did like having them out after dark. These streets are too narrow."

Even Magic and Moonshine seemed quite glad to get back, and Uncle Arthur said that he hoped Mrs Randall would not be away long.

There was no sign of Uncle Arthur's assistant next morning either, and Ian was sent round to inquire how she was. The news was not very promising.

"Her daughter came to the door, and she says Mrs Randall's still in bed," Ian told Uncle Arthur when he got back. "She doesn't think her mother will be back this week, anyway."

"Oh, my goodness." Uncle Arthur ran his fingers through his hair until it stood up in a grey bush. "What are we going to do?"

"I'm sure we could manage them on our own," said Ian. "Couldn't we try?"

"Oh dear. I don't like asking you to take so much responsibility." Their uncle looked unhappy. "I suppose it is the only way, though. I can't let my customers down by closing the shop. All right. But do be very, very careful, won't you?"

The children promised that they would be, and Uncle Arthur told them exactly where to go. This was round all the quietest streets in the district, and should not take them more than half an hour.

"And tomorrow we'll give them a really

good run during the afternoon," said Uncle Arthur.

He put on the ponies' bridles, and clipped a leading rein to each pony's bit. Then he fussed around them, brushing pieces of straw out of their tails, and cleaning the dirt out of their hooves. He obviously hated to let them go out without him. He was still tidying them when the shop bell clanged distantly inside the house.

"Now remember, walk one behind the other," he warned the children. "Keep between them and the traffic. Let Magic go first —he likes to see where he's going. Ian, you're taking Magic, aren't you, and Angela's having Moonshine."

"You there, Arthur?" shouted a distant voice. "Shop."

"Shall we go?" asked Ian.

"Yes, yes, go on then. Be back in half an hour, won't you? You've got my watch, Ian," said Uncle Arthur.

"Arthur," shouted the voice again, and Uncle Arthur had to go. Ian opened the gate, and he and Angela led the ponies out into the path.

Magic looked back once as though he was wondering where his master was, but after that he and Moonshine accepted the children as being in charge of them. At the end of the path they turned left down the road, and left again almost at once. This brought them into the very quiet road which was on the other side of the houses behind Uncle Arthur's. Jane and her brothers lived here, and so did some of Magic and Moonshine's other fans. They would be at school today, or so Ian and Angela thought.

But as the ponies went past the door of number eleven, where Jane lived, it opened, and she came out. One of her younger brothers, Dan, was with her, and her older brother, Alan, whom the children did not know very well, was also there.

"Where's your uncle?" inquired Jane at once.

"He's looking after the shop," replied Angela. "Mrs Randall's ill."

"Have you got a holiday?" asked Ian.

"No. Simon's got chickenpox, so Mum thought we'd better all stay at home," replied Jane.

Her older brother, who was a year or so older than Ian, was staring at the ponies with his hands in his pockets.

"Fancy him letting you take them out," he remarked. "I didn't think old Uncle Arthur ever trusted his precious ponies with anyone else."

"He does us," retorted Ian, who did not like the look of Alan.

"They're sweet," Jane was patting Moonshine. "Can we come with you?" she asked.

"I suppose so," said Ian unwillingly. Jane and Daniel were all right, but he did not like the idea of Alan coming along.

The street came to a dead end, but there was a narrow footpath through to the next street. Magic and Moonshine followed Ian and Angela between the posts that were meant to keep out cars, and Jane, Dan, and Alan brought up the rear.

100

7 · A stupid thing to do

It was a cold, sunny day, and the muddy garden in the middle of the square that they had come into looked quite green. Alan climbed the railings and jumped down inside the garden, but Jane and Daniel stayed beside the ponies.

"Why don't you let them walk side by side?" asked Jane. "That's how Mr Perry always leads them, one on each side."

"Uncle Arthur told us to keep them one behind the other," explained Angela. "It's safer if a car comes."

"I bet he told you everything," said Alan, arriving beside them again. "Where to go, how long to be, how many breaths to take. I thought they were supposed to be clever. If they're that clever they ought to be able to take themselves for a walk. They wouldn't

101

need a couple of kids tagging on."

"That's stupid," retorted Ian. "They are clever, but they're still ponies. They don't do their tricks on their own. They have to be told what to do."

"Can you make them do tricks?" asked Jane.

"Uncle Arthur showed us how," replied Ian, warily.

"He's never shown us," said Jane, rather jealously. "And we were here the first day he brought them home. Mum said she thought they'd smell, but at least they wouldn't bark all night, like the dog he used to have."

"They don't smell," exclaimed Angela.

"No, not really," agreed Jane. "Even Mum says they don't often. Only if it's very hot."

"I bet you can't make them do their tricks, even if you do know how," said Alan, who was bored with the conversation.

"We've never tried," Ian told him.

They had reached the end of the square now, and were going along the other side.

"Haven't you even tried to make them shake hands?" asked Jane. "Oh, do. I'm sure they would. Mr Perry always makes them shake hands with us when we go to see them."

"They can't," jeered Alan. "I expect they only do it for old Uncle Arthur Perry because they're scared of him. Mrs Crosbie at number fifteen says all performing animals are trained by cruelty."

"That's not true," cried Angela. "Uncle Arthur would never be cruel to any animal. All you do is this." She stopped Moonshine, stood in front of him, and held out her hand.

"Come on, Moonshine. Shake hands," she said.

Moonshine did as he was told, raising one forefoot, and holding it out to be shaken.

"You see?" said Angela. "And he couldn't be frightened of me, could he?"

"I don't see why not," said Alan darkly, but Jane was praising Angela, and saying how clever Moonshine was.

"You see?" she said. "You can make them

do things. Oh, please do. Go on, Ian, make Magic do something. It can't do any harm, surely."

It was very tempting. After all, Uncle Arthur had not said that they mustn't make the ponies do their tricks, and it would show Alan that they were not merely "kids" tagging along with the ponies. Also, Ian liked Jane and her smaller brother, and he knew that she really did want to see the ponies do some tricks.

Angela guessed what Ian was thinking, and felt worried. Although she had started it by making Moonshine shake hands she did not think that Uncle Arthur would like them playing about with the ponies' training.

"I don't think they really do know how," said Alan, who was getting tired of Angela and Ian and the ponies. He would go and find something else to do in a moment, he decided.

"I'm sure they do, really," insisted Jane. She could see that Ian was wavering, and it would be such fun if he stopped being stuffy and let them all play properly with the ponies. "Go on, Ian, please. Just make Magic do something. Make him push you, like he does Donnie Shaw on the stage."

There did not seem to be any possible harm in the idea, and Ian gave in.

"All right," he said. "Just once. Come on, Magic."

He turned his back to Magic as they had seen Uncle Arthur do, and began to pat Moonshine. Then he put one hand behind his back. Magic looked at him for a moment as though he was wondering if Ian really meant it. Then he took a step forward, and gave him a firm push. Daniel squealed with delight, and Jane laughed and clapped. Even Alan looked slightly impressed.

"Again," pleaded Jane. "Go on, Ian,"

Ian did it again, and for the second time Magic pushed him obediently. It was an exciting feeling, knowing that the pony would obey him so easily. Ian began to enjoy himself.

"Make him chase you," urged Jane.

"Do you think we ought?" asked Angela anxiously.

"I suppose it really can't do any harm," said Ian. After all, he thought, Uncle Arthur made the ponies do some of their tricks when they were out for exercise. The square was very quiet, traffic hardly ever seemed to come this way, and there did not seem to be any danger. The few parked cars were almost always there, no one ever seemed to take them for a drive, and some of them were clearly abandoned, with flat tyres and missing wings and windscreens, and there were no delivery vans about.

Ian decided that it was safe, hooked Magic's leading rein through the bridle, and moved away, leaving the pony loose. He kept one hand behind him, and Magic followed immediately, and gave him another push. Ian pretended to be indignant, and walked faster. Magic broke into a trot, and even Angela laughed at his ferocious expression.

Jane and Daniel were urging Magic on,

and Alan began to grin. Magic flattened his ears more closely to his head, and poked out his nose. Encouraged by their success, both he and Ian were beginning to get excited. Ian dodged on to the pavement, and Magic hopped up the curb after him. Ian jumped down again between two of the parked cars, and Magic dived after him.

"Quick, Ian; he nearly had you," cried Jane.

"Go on, Magic," shouted Alan.

Ian dodged round the front of one of the abandoned cars, and Magic, determined to catch up with him, broke into a canter. He whipped closely round the bonnet of the decrepit old car in pursuit.

There was a sudden hollow bang as the pony collided with the wing of the car, a squeal from Magic, and a rending noise. Then Magic was standing on the pavement, holding up one hind leg from which blood was dripping. The rusty front bumper of the car hung down to the road where Magic had ripped it off.

"Oh, Ian, look," wailed Angela.

"Oh, Ian, look what he's done," gasped Jane.

"Gosh, look at that," exclaimed Alan, in an awed voice.

Daniel burst into noisy tears, and Jane picked him up. Ian and Angela looked at one another, and at Magic, in frozen silence. Ian's face was very white, and Angela thought that she might be going to be sick.

Magic put his hind foot gingerly to the ground, and Ian took hold of his leading rein. The blood was still trickling down the inside of the pony's leg from somewhere above the bent part that was called the hock. His pale, creamy hair was turning dark and sticky, and there seemed to be a lot of blood on the pavement.

Moonshine watched the scene with pricked ears, looking surprised by the sudden air of trouble. Magic half-pricked his own ears, and decided that he was still interested in his reward for doing his trick. He began to sniff at Ian's pockets.

"He wants his carrot," whispered Jane.

She was almost as white as Ian and Angela, and her eyes were enormous. Even Alan looked shaken, and Daniel was still crying, though more quietly now.

"Have you got one?" Ian asked Angela. His voice sounded queer, and Angela knew that he felt as awful as she did. She found a piece of carrot in her pocket, and Magic ate it quite happily.

"What shall we do?" asked Angela shakily. "Do you think he can walk home?"

"It doesn't seem to be hurting him very much," said Ian. "We'd better try."

"We'll come too," said Jane. "After all, it was our fault for wanting to see him do tricks."

"Yes. We were a bit stupid," said Alan bluntly. "Come on, let's all go and face old Uncle Arthur."

"I was the most stupid of all," said Ian miserably. "I knew I shouldn't do it, but I went on."

He led Magic off the pavement, and the pony followed stiffly. He was not very lame, however, and the blood did not seem to be running terribly fast. Slowly and sadly they started towards home, Jane, Daniel, and Alan trailing behind, and Ian and Angela not daring to imagine what Uncle Arthur was going to say.

Uncle Arthur had been watching for them, and he came down the kitchen steps as they opened the gate. He saw at once that something was wrong, and it only took him a moment to spot Magic's leg.

"Whatever have you been doing?" he demanded. "What happened? Oh my goodness, what a mess. Give him to me, Ian."

All the children began to explain at once, but Uncle Arthur was hardly listening. He knelt down to examine Magic's injury, and told Angela to put Moonshine in the stable.

"It was our fault really; we wanted to see Magic do some tricks," said Jane.

"Ian, fetch me some hot water from the kettle," instructed Uncle Arthur. "Bring it in a clean basin. And bring the first aid box as well. Then you can telephone the vet—his number's on the card."

"We were a bit stupid," said Alan. "But it seemed all right round there."

"Yes, all right. I don't want to hear it all

111

now," replied Uncle Arthur shortly. "It's done and now it's got to be dealt with. You three had better go home. Off with you, now."

Jane, Alan and Daniel knew better than to argue. They let themselves rather thankfully out of the gate. Inside the stable Angela stayed where she was. She could not bear to face Uncle Arthur at the moment.

Ian brought the water and the white box marked with its red cross, and Uncle Arthur poured disinfectant into the bowl. He got out the cotton wool. Ian hurried back into the house to telephone the vet.

"Angela," called her uncle. "Come and hold Magic, please."

Timidly, Angela did as she was told. Ian came back after a few minutes to say that the vet was on his way. Then he stood miserably watching while Uncle Arthur bathed the cut, and washed away the drying blood from Magic's leg. The pony flinched slightly as the disinfectant stung the cut, but he did not try to kick or move away. His patience made Angela feel even worse. How could they have let him hurt himself?

"Well," said Uncle Arthur eventually, "can't do much more until the vet comes. You two go indoors. It won't help, all of us hanging around watching."

In Uncle Arthur's crowded living-room Angela and Ian looked at each other unhappily.

"Do you think Magic will be all right?" whispered Angela.

"I hope so," replied Ian. "After all, it is only a cut." He did not feel as confident as he sounded, but he wanted to reassure Angela.

"Uncle Arthur won't want us to come to stay again now," said Angela miserably. "Or live here, if there ever is a chance. Though I don't suppose there will be."

She sat down in the armchair by the fire, clasping her arms round her knees, and pressing her chin against them. Her long fair hair fell forward, hiding her face, and Ian knew that she was really wretched. She only sat like that when something went really

113

wrong, such as the time when they heard Uncle Sam say that they would be better put in a Home, and the time when Aunt Mavis took the stray kitten that they had found and gave it to the pet shop. It made Ian feel horribly guilty, for this time he was the main cause of the unhappiness. If only he had been more sensible.

The vet came, and only stayed for a few minutes. After he had gone Uncle Arthur came into the house.

"What did the vet say?" asked Angela anxiously.

"He thinks Magic should be all right in a few days," replied Uncle Arthur. "He gave him an anti-tetanus injection, and said the cut didn't seem very bad. He was in a hurry —he had an emergency to go to somewhere else."

"I really am most frightfully sorry," said Ian. "It was all my fault. I just didn't see how it could hurt to have him do some of his tricks. Jane really did want to see them."

"Oh, it's not your fault," said Uncle Arthur,

rather vaguely. "Too much responsibility for you. I shouldn't have asked you to do it at your ages. It's my own fault for expecting too much. Hope Magic won't move around too much on that leg. I'd better pop out and have another look."

He went, leaving Ian staring miserably at the floor. So Uncle Arthur did not really blame him at all. He just thought him too young to behave sensibly. It hurt even more than Uncle Arthur being really cross would have done. And of course it made no difference to the future. Uncle Arthur would not want them again if he felt that they were merely irresponsible.

When Grace was told about the accident later she took a slightly different view. She said at once that Ian was old enough to have had more sense. She also said that she was sure Magic would be perfectly all right in a day or two.

"It doesn't even matter if it leaves a scar," she pointed out to Uncle Arthur. "It won't show on the inside of his leg. And as there aren't any tendons or anything damaged I can't see that any of you need to worry. He's a healthy young animal, and it'll soon heal."

She went on firmly to talk about something else, and by the time she went home they were all feeling a lot more cheerful. Uncle Arthur even got out the Snakes and Ladders board for a game before bed, and the cloud which had hung over them all afternoon no longer seemed half as heavy.

8 · A real home

Magic seemed as bright as usual next day, although Uncle Arthur said that his leg seemed rather hot. He was not supposed to walk much, although he could wander round the yard to stretch his legs a little.

As it was early closing day Uncle Arthur took Moonshine out for half an hour after lunch, leaving instructions that neither of the children was to touch Magic while he was gone. It was not nice to know that they were not trusted, and Angela and Ian stayed in the house, attempting to play draughts, although they did not feel at all like it.

Magic did not finish his evening feed. There was not a lot left, but enough to worry Uncle Arthur.

"Always loves his food," he told the children anxiously. "Oh dear. That leg is hot.

Can't call the vet at this time unless I'm sure."

Magic nuzzled his hand, and accepted a carrot, and Uncle Arthur's anxiety faded a little. He decided to wait and see how Magic was next morning.

Angela did not sleep very well that night, and several times she heard Uncle Arthur get up and creep down the stairs and out into the yard to look at Magic. By the time she and Ian went down next morning it was obvious that something was wrong. The pony did not want any of his breakfast, and his leg was hot and swollen, with the infection running right up his leg. Uncle Arthur went indoors to telephone the vet, and to start making a bran mash to encourage Magic to eat.

When the vet came he agreed that an infection had developed from the cut.

"There may have been a scrap of metal left in it," he said. "Or the piece he cut himself on may have been very dirty. I'll give him a penicillin injection, and open the wound again. That should drain it and get

118

rid of the trouble. He has a temperature, so don't let him get cold and give him plenty of chilled water and warm mashes. If he won't eat he might drink skimmed milk with a little water."

"Do you think he'll come through it all right?" asked Uncle Arthur anxiously.

"Oh, there's no reason why he shouldn't,"

replied the vet. "But he'll need a bit of care. I'll call tomorrow and see how he is."

Magic was certainly not very happy. After the vet had gone Uncle Arthur found an extra blanket for him to wear under his rug, and put extra straw down in his stall. He stirred up the cooled mash, and offered that to the pony, but Magic was not interested. Uncle Arthur tried warmed water, and the pony took a few mouthfuls of that. While Uncle Arthur was busy with Magic the shop bell clanged.

"Oh dear, Ian, you go, will you?" said Uncle Arthur.

Ian did so, and managed to weigh out a quarter of fruit drops, and take the right money. Then he went back to the stable.

Magic looked very miserable. His thick, soft coat looked harsh, and the hairs were standing on end. His usually bright eyes were dull and half-closed, and obviously his leg was hurting him. In the other half of the shed Moonshine watched curiously. Now and then he made soft, snuffling noises, asking for attention himself, and Angela rubbed his ears and patted him.

"I'll stay with Magic," said Uncle Arthur. "He shouldn't be left alone in this state. Besides, if he lies down his bad leg will make it hard for him to get up. You two keep away. Best if he's as quiet as possible. If he doesn't improve we'll have Moonshine out in the yard. Rig up some cover for him. He won't hurt there for a night or two."

Angela and Ian went back into the house. The remains of breakfast were still on the table, and it was almost lunch time. The bell clanged in the shop as they went inside, and Ian said, "I'd better go. I don't expect Uncle Arthur will want to come."

"I wish Mrs Randall was back," said Angela. "And I do hope Grace comes round today."

"She often doesn't come on a Thursday," replied Ian. "And she is extra busy this week because of the dancing school's exams."

There were impatient shuffling and coughing sounds coming from the shop, and Ian went through to serve the customer. Angela began to clear away the breakfast things. She very much hoped that Grace would find time to come round that day.

Magic was certainly no better that evening. Grace had not been round, and Uncle Arthur had only been into the house to fetch milk and warm water for Magic, or to find tit-bits with which to tempt the pony. He had not even stayed inside to eat his lunch, and Angela had taken some out to him on a tray. Even then he had hardly touched it.

Ian had looked after the shop, without making any serious mistakes, and Angela made all the beds, washed up, and cooked. Several customers asked Ian where Uncle Arthur was, but Ian just said that he was busy outside. He was not very eager for the whole district to know about the accident.

Uncle Arthur came into the house while Angela was getting the tea. He looked grimy and tired, and he had not shaved that day.

"I'm going to put Moonshine outside," he said. "I don't want Magic disturbed if he

122

does rest tonight. Ian, come and help, will you?"

There was an old tarpaulin in the loft, and Ian helped his uncle to get it down. They carried it into the yard, and with Ian's help Uncle Arthur fixed one side to the roof of the shed. From there he slung it across to the fence, and he fastened the other corner by a rope to the roof of the bathroom. This made a three-sided shelter for Moonshine, one side being the shed wall, the second the back fence, and the third the loose flap of the tarpaulin. Uncle Arthur anchored this to the ground by putting two bales of hay on the edge where it touched the yard. Then he and Ian spread thick straw under it for Moonshine's bed, and Uncle Arthur fetched the pony out.

Moonshine did not seem to mind his temporary stable. He was tethered to a ring in the fence, with his tail to the open side of the shelter, and given plenty of hay. He began to munch straight away. Magic hardly seemed to have noticed him going.

123

"What about your tea?" asked Ian, when Uncle Arthur turned to go back into the stable.

"Oh, Angela can bring me something out here," replied Uncle Arthur. "Mind you two eat something, though. And then get to bed. I shall be staying with Magic, so don't wait."

Ian and Angela ate their tea almost without speaking. After they had cleared away Angela went out to get Uncle Arthur's tray. She also took him some more hot water to make Magic a fresh poultice and to add to bran to try him with another mash. The shed door was closed, but Moonshine whinnied softly to her from his place under the tarpaulin.

At Angela's soft tap Uncle Arthur opened the door and gave her the tray. She handed him the kettle of hot water.

Inside the shed the light was on, but shaded by a piece of sacking, and Magic stood miserably in the shadows with his head hanging down.

"Shh," hissed Uncle Arthur, when she started to speak. "You and Ian go to bed."

124

"You haven't eaten your tea," Angela whispered.

"Never mind," Uncle Arthur whispered back. "It won't hurt me to go without. I'll fetch something later if he seems better."

He closed the door, and Angela took the tray indoors.

"He didn't eat much dinner either," she told Ian. "He must be awfully worried."

Ian nodded. He felt more guilty than ever, but there was nothing at all that he and Angela could do to help get the pony better. If only, thought Ian for the hundredth time, it had never happened.

Ian and Angela were already awake when Uncle Arthur came into the house next morning to get the papers ready for delivery. They went downstairs in their dressing gowns to ask how Magic was, but they knew at once from his face that the pony was no better.

"But he isn't any worse," Uncle Arthur told them. "That's something, my goodness it is."

He yawned, shivered, and pulled his coat

125

more closely round him.

"Very cold this morning," he said.

"I'll make some tea," said Angela.

Uncle Arthur looked cold; his hair was standing on end, and his eyes were red from staying awake all night. Ian went to help with the papers, and Angela put the kettle on. She felt very worried. Uncle Arthur looked as though he, too, might be ill if he had to sit with Magic much longer.

The papers were ready very quickly that morning, and Uncle Arthur swallowed a cup of tea before hurrying back to the stable. The vet called just after breakfast, as he had promised to do, and said that it was a good sign that the pony was no worse.

"Oughtn't we to tell Grace what's happened?" Ian asked Uncle Arthur, when the vet had gone. "She could help you with Magic, couldn't she?"

"Dear me, no," exclaimed Uncle Arthur. "You're not to go bothering Grace. She's been more than good. I can't possibly ask her to do anything more. Besides, she's got

126

enough to do this week, with those exams to play for. And I couldn't ask a lady like Grace to sit out in the stable. As for the shop, if it gets too difficult I'll shut for a day or two. If you have any real problems there, come out and ask me. But don't make a noise."

He hurried out with a fresh kettle of warm water, and Angela and Ian looked at each other helplessly.

"I wish he'd let one of us sit with Magic for a bit," said Angela. "But he won't trust us."

"I don't blame him, after what happened the last time he did," replied Ian gloomily.

Already, the house looked a mess. Uncle Arthur might not seem to do any housework, but he was clever at putting things back where they came from, and clearing up any litter he made before he started to do something else. He would flick over the sideboard with a duster while he was talking, and sweep up the hearth each time he rebuilt the fire.

Now, everything looked dusty, and the hearth was thick with cinders and ash. The fire was not burning very well because it had not been properly riddled, and several drawers were partly open where they had searched hurriedly for something. There were crumbs on the floor around the table, and Partner's milk had been spilt on the kitchen floor, and not wiped up.

Drearily, in between washing up and cooking, and serving in the shop, Ian and Angela tried to clear up a bit. Once or twice, as she struggled with a carpet-sweeper that needed emptying, and as Ian tried unsuccessfully to get the fire burning properly, Angela almost found herself wishing them back with Aunt Mavis. It was all so difficult, and she had a terrible feeling that Magic was not going to get better, and that Uncle Arthur would never forgive them. Their dreams of staying with him again, or perhaps even living at the shop, seemed very far away now, and very impossible. This was not their real life, and never could be now that they had made such a mess of things.

The afternoon dragged past. At about five o'clock, though time was vague because the clock had stopped, Angela took some tea out to the stable. Uncle Arthur opened the door at her knock, but to her alarm he did not seem able to stand up properly.

"All right. Nothing much. Cramp," he explained, seeing her scared expression. "Been sitting too long."

"How's Magic?" asked Angela timidly.

"Oh, about the same," replied her uncle. "About the same. You two managing all right?"

"Yes, we're all right," Angela assured him. "You will eat some tea, won't you, Uncle?"

"Yes, don't worry about me. Go on now, don't want to disturb him," said Uncle Arthur.

Ian came in from the shop as Angela returned. He looked flushed and cross, and explained that he had just given someone the wrong change.

"She was awfully cross," he said. "I think

she thought I'd done it on purpose. She wasn't a regular customer."

"Oh dear," Angela sat sadly down at the table. "It's all so awful."

"Jane came in, too," said Ian. "She wanted to know how Magic was."

Angela nodded. It was kind of Jane to worry. It seemed as though Jane was probably rather nice. But she was too miserable to be really interested.

After tea they discovered that the fire had gone out completely. Partner, disgusted, was curled up deep in an armchair with his nose in his tail. There was no hot water to do the washing up. Then Angela picked up the tea pot to clear away, the handle came off, and the half-full pot fell to the floor, flooding the carpet with tea. It was too much. Angela flung herself on to the settee, and burst into tears.

"Angela," exclaimed a voice from the door. "What on earth's the matter? Whatever has been happening?" and to Ian's great relief Grace walked into the room. She sat down beside Angela and put her arms round her, and Ian began to explain.

"But why didn't one of you come and tell me?" asked Grace. "I'm never that busy."

"Uncle Arthur said we weren't to bother you," sobbed Angela. "He said you'd been more than good, and anyway, he couldn't ask a lady like you to sit out in the stable. Oh, Aunt Grace, Magic looks awful, I'm sure he's going to die, and Uncle Arthur looks as if he's getting ill as well."

"Honestly," exclaimed Grace. "Sometimes, I despair of Arthur. Now, stop crying, Angela. I'll go out and talk to him. I'm sure it isn't that bad. I can stay with Magic while Arthur gets some sleep. I expect that's all he needs. As for Magic, he's a tough little animal, and I don't see any reason why he should die."

She left her basket on the kitchen table and went out into the yard. Angela and Ian waited anxiously, Angela still sniffling, and Ian staring out of the window. For about five minutes nothing happened, and then Ian saw the stable door open.

"Uncle Arthur's coming out," he exclaimed. "And Grace."

"Do you think he's going to let her help?" asked Angela anxiously.

"I don't know," replied Ian.

"Angela," called Grace, from the kitchen. "Heat your Uncle some milk, and see that he has some rum in it. And fill a hot water bottle for him. I'm going back to sit with Magic. I'll take his milk and some water for another mash with me."

"He won't take it," said Uncle Arthur dully. He sat down on a kitchen chair. Grace re-lit the fire on top of the warm ashes.

"Sit by the fire," she instructed. "And stop worrying. He'll take a bit. He doesn't look that bad to me, and you said yourself he'd been nosing in his straw."

"You'll call me if he gets worse, won't you? said Uncle Arthur.

"I've promised I will," replied Grace. "Now drink that milk and go to bed. I'm going back to the pony."

She went out, taking the bucket of milk

and water and a saucepan of hot water with her.

"Is Magic a bit better?" asked Angela, as her Uncle drank his hot milk and rum.

"Possibly. Just a bit," replied Uncle Arthur. "Might not last, though. I hope Grace can manage. If he lies down, he won't be able to stand up again without help; leg's too swollen. Very good of her to try to help."

He went slowly up to bed at last, leaving the children to clear up as best they could. But they did feel slightly more cheerful as they went up to bed themselves.

Angela and Ian were woken the next morning by the sound of the back door closing very softly. Uncle Arthur was still asleep; they could hear him snoring slightly as they crept downstairs. Grace was in the kitchen, filling the kettle. She looked tired, but cheerful, and Ian said, "How's Magic?"

"Come and see," replied Grace. "Put your coats on. It's cold."

They followed her down the steps, feeling the frost rime cold and suddenly melting on the rail as they touched it. Moonshine was munching in his shelter, and Grace opened the shed door. An eager whinny greeted them, and Magic turned to face them, his head up and his ears pricked. His eyes were bright again, and his coat was no longer rough and staring. The only signs that he had been ill were some swelling still in his leg, and a hollow look about his neck just past the end of his rug. Clearly, his leg no longer hurt him, and his temperature had gone down.

"He's better," cried Angela.

"Yes," agreed Grace. "I don't think we shall need to worry about him much more."

Ian said nothing, but his face as he patted Magic was one broad grin. Then Magic raised his head sharply and gave a little whinny, and Ian and Angela turned round to see Uncle Arthur, wearing his dressing gown, standing in the doorway.

"My goodness, Grace, what did you do? Wave your magic wand?" exclaimed Uncle Arthur. "He looks terrific."

"I thought he seemed to be brighter than you thought last night," replied Grace. "He ate a bit of the mash I took him, and he lay down to sleep. I had to help him up a bit this morning, but after that he wanted hay and breakfast, and to be played with. I didn't have to do anything for him in the night. I even got some sleep."

"Well, that's marvellous. Marvellous," said Uncle Arthur. He rubbed Magic's ears, and patted him, until Moonshine called to remind them that he was being left out.

"He could come back in here now, couldn't he?" asked Grace, and Uncle Arthur agreed that he could.

Ian fetched him in, and Magic greeted his friend with a loud whinny.

"Well," said Grace. "I think we could all go in for breakfast now, don't you?"

Magic continued to get better steadily during the next few days, and by the middle of the next week he was able to go for his usual outings, although he was still a bit stiff. Jane and her brothers were as delighted

135

as anyone to see him about again, and they and Angela and Ian accepted each other as friends in a way they had not done before the accident.

In spite of Magic's recovery, however, and the general cheerfulness, Ian and Angela grew quieter as the days passed. It could not possibly be long now before Aunt Mavis was ready to have them home. Already they had stayed longer than her last letter had suggested. Grace looked at them sometimes, and asked a few questions about life with their aunt.

Although they tried to be fair when they replied, they could not help showing that they were not looking forward to going back to Surbiton.

Since Magic's illness Grace was careful to come round every day. She obviously felt partly to blame for the state that they had got into when she did not know that there was anything wrong. Once or twice she and Uncle Arthur stopped talking rather quickly when Ian or Angela came into the room.

Ian hoped that it was not the accident that they were discussing. He still felt very guilty about that, although Magic was obviously going to be as sound and well as ever.

Then, at lunchtime on Saturday, when Grace was there as well, Uncle Arthur said that Aunt Mavis had written to him, and was coming home.

"She says she can have you back about the middle of the week," he told them. "She'll be home and have everything straight by then."

"Oh. I see." Ian looked down at his plate.

Angela said nothing. She knew that she would not be able to swallow any more dinner, and that if she said anything she would cry.

It was all over, the busy, exciting, sometimes hectic time at Uncle Arthur's. The feeling of really belonging somewhere, and with someone, was over, and Angela knew that she had never been happier anywhere.

"There is one possible alternative," said Grace. "One thing you could do instead."

She looked at Uncle Arthur, who cleared his throat and went rather red.

"Yes," he said. "Well. The thing is, Grace and I have decided to get married. I need

someone to keep me in order, and she says she doesn't mind trying. If you'd like it, she's willing to try to keep you two in order as well. And I'd certainly miss your help with Magic and Moonshine, not to mention

Angela's cooking. But of course, it's entirely up to you."

"We have mentioned the idea to your aunt," went on Grace. "Arthur suggested that there might be more scope for your energy here, as your aunt leads such a busy life, and has such a lovely home. What do you think? Would you like to live here properly?"

"Like it?" cried Angela. Her face was crimson, and her eyes shone. "Oh, Aunt Grace, we'd love it. Please. We really have been so happy here."

"Are you sure?" asked Ian, more quietly. "I mean, even after the accident?"

"Accidents can always happen," replied Uncle Arthur. "And I don't suppose you'd let that kind happen twice. Of course we're sure. It'd seem jolly quiet and dull here without you."

"Then we would like to stay. I can't think of anything we'd like better," said Ian joyfully.

For a few minutes there was chaos, while

Angela rushed round the table to hug both Uncle Arthur and Grace, and Ian leaped up to perform a war dance.

Partner shot up on top of the sideboard at all the noise, and Bluey began to screech in competition.

"Don't forget there'll be school now," warned Grace, but they were not at all dampened.

"I've got jobs lined up for you both already," said Uncle Arthur, when things had quietened down a little. "Grace and I will need a bridesmaid, and a footman to hold the ponies while we're in church."

"The ponies?" exclaimed Angela. "Will you take Magic and Moonshine to the wedding, then?"

"Of course," replied Uncle Arthur, looking shocked. "Couldn't leave them out. I know where I can get a beautiful little carriage for them, just the right size."

"Oh, Arthur," exclaimed Grace, laughing. "And Partner too, as coachman?"

"Why not?" asked Uncle Arthur. "Why

not? It's an idea, Grace. I might even try it."

And while everyone laughed Angela and Ian caught one another's eyes, and exchanged a private grin of complete satisfaction. Everything was all right now. They had found a real and permanent home at last.

Also by Gillian Baxter

SAVE THE PONIES!

Angela and Ian are dismayed when Uncle Arthur has to consider selling Magic and Moonshine – but the ponies themselves provide the answer to the problem!

This is the second exciting book about Magic and Moonshine, the pantomime ponies.

PONIES BY THE SEA

Angela and Ian are delighted when their pantomime ponies, Magic and Moonshine, are booked for a summer show and the whole family are to go to the seaside for six weeks!

But the holiday starts badly for Angela as Ian makes friends with some other children and she is left out. She spends a lot of time with the ponies in their orchard – and discovers that they have a mysterious visitor who doesn't want to be seen . . .

This is the third exciting book about Magic and Moonshine, the pantomime ponies.

Ponies in Harness, the fourth book about Magic and Moonshine, is also available from Mammoth.

A Selected List of Fiction from Mammoth

While every effort is made to keep prices low, it is sometimes necessary to increase prices at short notice. Mandarin Paperbacks reserves the right to show new retail prices on covers which may differ from those previously advertised in the text or elsewhere.

The prices shown below were correct at the time of going to press.

☐	7497 1409 3	**Not Just Dancing**	Helen Flint	£2.99
☐	7497 1073 X	**Dying to Win**	Eileen Goudge	£2.99
☐	7497 0487 X	**Wait Till Helen Comes**	Mary Downing Hahn	£2.99
☐	7497 1460 3	**The Dead Hour**	Pete Johnson	£3.50
☐	7497 0281 8	**The Homeward Bounders**	Diana Wynne Jones	£3.50
☐	7497 1265 1	**Mandragora**	David McRobbie	£3.50
☐	7497 1061 6	**A Little Love Song**	Michelle Magorian	£3.99
☐	7497 1482 4	**Writing in Martian**	Andrew Matthews	£2.99
☐	7497 0323 7	**Silver**	Norma Fox Mazer	£3.50
☐	7497 0325 3	**The Girl of his Dreams**	Harry Mazer	£2.99
☐	7497 0280 X	**Beyond the Labyrinth**	Gillian Rubinstein	£2.50
☐	7497 0558 2	**Frankie's Story**	Catherine Sefton	£2.99
☐	7497 1291 0	**The Spirit House**	William Sleator	£2.99
☐	7497 0764 X	**Pebble on the Beach**	Ian Strachan	£2.99
☐	7497 0009 2	**Secret Diary of Adrian Mole**	Sue Townsend	£3.50
☐	7497 1015 2	**Come Lucky April**	Jean Ure	£2.99
☐	7497 0147 1	**A Walk on the Wild Side**	Robert Westall	£3.50

All these books are available at your bookshop or newsagent, or can be ordered direct from the address below. Just tick the titles you want and fill in the form below.

Cash Sales Department, PO Box 5, Rushden, Northants NN10 6YX.
Fax: 0933 410321 : Phone 0933 410511.

Please send cheque, payable to 'Reed Book Services Ltd.', or postal order for purchase price quoted and allow the following for postage and packing:

£1.00 for the first book, 50p for the second; **FREE POSTAGE AND PACKING FOR THREE BOOKS OR MORE PER ORDER.**

NAME (Block letters) ....

ADDRESS ....

....

☐ I enclose my remittance for ....

☐ I wish to pay by Access/Visa Card Number ☐☐☐☐☐☐☐☐☐☐☐☐☐☐☐☐

Expiry Date ☐☐☐☐

Signature ....

Please quote our reference: MAND